SMITHSONIAN

U.S. CAPITOL

HOTEL

THE WORST CLASS TRIP EVER

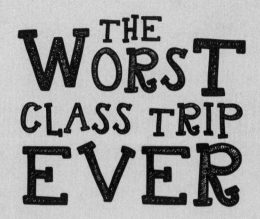

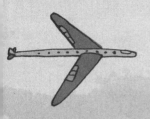

ALSO BY DAVE BARRY

With Ridley Pearson

Peter and the Starcatchers

Peter and the Shadow Thieves

Peter and the Secret of Rundoon

Peter and the Sword of Mercy

Bridge to Never Land

Science Fair

THE WORST CLASS TRIP EVER

DAVE BARRY

ILLUSTRATED BY JON CANNELL

Disney • HYPERION

LOS ANGELES   NEW YORK

Text copyright © 2015 by Dave Barry
Illustrations copyright © 2015 by Jon Cannell

Printed in the United States of America
Reinforced binding

First Edition, May 2015
10 9 8 7 6 5 4 3 2 1

G475-5664-5-15046

Library of Congress Cataloging-in-Publication Data

Barry, Dave.
The Worst class trip ever / by Dave Barry.—First edition.
pages cm
Summary: When the eighth grade civics class of Miami's Culver Middle
School goes on a trip to Washington, D.C., Wyatt Palmer finds himself in deep
trouble before the plane even lands because his best friend, Matt, has decided
the men sitting behind them are terrorists and it is up to the boys to stop them.
ISBN 978-1-4847-0849-1
[1. School field trips—Fiction. 2. Conduct of life—Fiction. 3. Terrorism—
Fiction. 4. Washington (D.C.)—Fiction. 5. Humorous stories.] I. Title.
PZ7.B278Wor 2015
[Fic]—dc23   2014013171

Visit www.DisneyBooks.com

SUSTAINABLE   Certified Sourcing
FORESTRY
INITIATIVE   www.sfiprogram.org
              SFI-00993

THIS LABEL APPLIES TO TEXT STOCK

For Dylan Maxwell Barry, a whole new generation

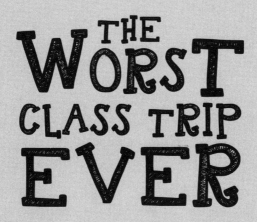

THE WORST CLASS TRIP EVER

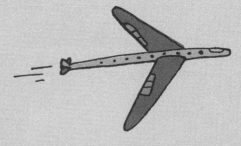

CHAPTER 1

None of this stuff would have happened if I hadn't been sitting next to Matthew Diaz.

Don't get me wrong: Matt is my best friend. But he can be an idiot. But when we were in kindergarten, pretty much *all* the boys were idiots, so he didn't stand out so much, and we became best friends. So now, even though we're in eighth grade, and he's sometimes unbelievably annoying, I'm kind of stuck with him.

That's why I ended up sitting next to him on the plane on the class trip. I think about that sometimes. If I'd been sitting anywhere else, I would have had a normal class trip, and none of this insane mess would have happened.

On the other hand, when I think about what could have happened if I *hadn't* been sitting next to Matt on that flight . . .

Okay, I guess this is starting to sound pretty mysterious. Let me start at the beginning:

My name is Wyatt Palmer. I'm an eighth grader at Culver Middle School in Miami. I know a lot of people think Miami is a weird place, but it's my home, so I'm used to the kind of things that happen there that don't happen in normal places.

Like there was this incident that happened about six months ago when my dad went outside to get the *Miami Herald* off our lawn. My dad likes to read the sports section while he has his coffee so he can complain about how much the Dolphins suck. So first thing every morning, he goes outside and gets the paper off the lawn.

For years he did this wearing only his boxers. My mom hated this. She was always telling my dad to at least put on a bathrobe, because what if somebody saw him. My dad said nobody's going to be out there at six thirty a.m., and besides wearing boxer shorts is the same as wearing a bathing suit. This is not really true, especially if you saw my dad's bedtime boxers, which have like zero elastic and a lot of holes and according to my mom are held together mainly by stains. A couple of times, she threw them away, but my dad went and got them out of the trash. He's very loyal to his boxers.

So anyway, this particular morning my dad went outside as usual to get the paper, and as usual our dog, Csonka, stood in the doorway to watch him. Csonka likes to keep an eye on things, but he knows he's not allowed to go outside without a leash. Anyway, my dad was out there, bending over to pick up the newspaper—trust me, you do *not* want to see that—and all of a sudden Csonka started barking like crazy. My dad jumped up and turned around, and he was about to yell at Csonka to shut up, when all of a sudden he saw what Csonka was barking at.

An alligator.

We live near a canal. There are canals all over Miami, and they connect to the Everglades, which means if you live here, you basically live in a swamp. I mean, we have houses and roads and shopping centers and stuff, but it's all built on top of a swamp, and as far as the swamp animals are concerned, it's still a swamp, and it's still theirs. It's normal for us to see snakes in our yards, and lizards, and all kinds of frogs, and big tall wading birds, and even crabs in some neighborhoods. And every now and then an alligator shows up.

This particular alligator, which was not a small alligator, was on our lawn maybe ten feet from our front walkway, which means my dad went right past without seeing it on his way to the newspaper. But he definitely saw it when Csonka started barking. And no way was he going to try to walk past it again.

He started yelling "Rosa! Rosa!" calling my mom. She and my sister, Taylor, and I all went running to the door to see what was going on. My dad was out on the sidewalk, holding up his boxers with one hand and using the other one to point the *Miami Herald* at the alligator, like it was a weapon or something. My mom screamed, and so did Taylor, and maybe I also made an unmanly noise, because it really was a pretty major alligator.

"CALL 911!" shouted my dad. "HURRY!"

"Okay!" said my mom, running to the kitchen.

By now Csonka was really going crazy barking. He was also out of the house, which was a violation of the leash rule, but I guess he figured he was protecting my dad. What he was really doing was upsetting the alligator, which started to move forward in that slow way alligators walk. I think it was going for Csonka, but it was moving kind of in the direction of Taylor and me, so my father came running down the walk, waving the *Miami Herald* toward the alligator and going, "Shoo! Get away!"

That was definitely the bravest thing I ever saw my dad do, but it did not impress the alligator. What it did was make the alligator turn more in the direction of my dad, who turned right around and went sprinting back toward the sidewalk.

"RUN IN A ZIGZAG PATTERN!" shouted Taylor.

The reason she shouted that was, in Florida, some people believe alligators can only run in a straight line, so they tell kids that if a gator is chasing them, they should run in a zigzag pattern. But it's a myth. In fifth grade my science teacher, Mrs. Buntz, showed us a video of an alligator chasing a dead chicken being dragged by a guy in a zigzag pattern, and the gator had no trouble following it. Mrs. Buntz said you should run in a straight line.

"THAT'S A MYTH!" I shouted to my dad. "RUN IN A STRAIGHT LINE!"

"Are you trying to *kill* him?" yelled Taylor, punching my arm. She's in sixth grade and very dramatic.

The truth was, my dad couldn't hear either of us, because of Csonka's barking, which was getting even louder. The alligator was now standing right on the walkway, and Csonka was getting pretty close to it, which was not good because alligators, besides being able to zigzag, can also move really fast when they want to. The one in Mrs. Buntz's video caught the chicken and almost caught the guy dragging it.

The police came pretty fast, three cars in like two minutes. They stopped in the street in front of our house with their lights flashing. All the neighbors came out of their houses to see what was going on. Also people on their way to work were stopping their cars to watch.

The police got out of their cars but didn't get too close to the alligator, which was still watching Csonka, who was still barking. So everybody just stood around for a few minutes, while more commuters stopped their cars, so by now there was a pretty big crowd out there with my dad.

Finally some animal-control officers showed up. They're used to alligators on people's lawns, and they handled this one in like five minutes. They snagged it with a noose, duct-taped its mouth shut, and took it away in a van. The neighbors went back inside, and the commuters drove away, and Csonka finally shut up, and it was all over except for my mom reminding my dad that she *told* him not to wear his boxers outside but did he listen? No! he did not listen, etc. etc. etc. like six hundred and fifty times.

That night, when we were eating dinner, I got a text from a kid in my class saying *chan 4 now lol*. So we turned on the kitchen TV and there was our house, in a cell phone video one of the commuters took. You could see the gator, and there was a nice close-up of my dad, holding up his holey boxers, with his belly sagging down and his hair sticking out every direction the way it does in the morning.

I said, "Real good look, Dad."

My dad said, "They can't show that without my permission, can they?"

Taylor said, "I'm gonna skip school for the rest of my life."

My mom didn't say anything, which is not like her. She's Cuban. She just stared at the TV until the alligator story was over. Then she got up and walked out of the kitchen. About a minute later we heard the patio door open and close. We went to look, and there was my mom on the patio next to the pool, standing over my dad's boxers.

Which were on fire.

When they were totally burned up, she splashed some pool water on the ashes and walked back into the house, right past my dad, not saying a word. I don't know if they talked about it later. I do know that the next morning, when he went out to get the paper, he wore a bathrobe.

But my point (I bet you forgot I had a point) is that stuff

like that—an alligator on the lawn—happens all the time in Miami. You get used to it, the way you get used to palm trees and hurricanes and hardly ever needing a sweater. Also you get used to hearing Spanish. Like my mom; she grew up in the U.S. and speaks English without an accent, but when her family's around—all the aunts and uncles and cousins, like seventeen thousand of them—she switches to Spanish. I grew up understanding it, and at Culver Middle School some of my classes are totally in Spanish. Other kids take classes in French and German. Culver is a language magnet school. What it's mainly a magnet for, if you want to know the truth, is nerds. But I'm basically a nerd myself—I admit it—so I like it.

And it turned out that being nerdy was pretty handy on the class trip.

The trip was for the Culver eighth-grade civics classes. Every year they go to Washington, D.C. This year there were forty-seven kids on the trip, plus two teachers and eight parent chaperones.

The teachers were Mr. Arnold Barto and Miss Christine Rector. Mr. Barto is my civics teacher, and he's a good enough guy, but he forgets stuff. I mean, a *lot* of stuff. Like, he'll say, "Today we're going to cover the Sixth Amendment to the Constitution." And we'll be like, "We already covered that." And he's like, "We did? When?" And we're like, "Last year, in seventh grade." And he's like, "Wait, you aren't seventh grade?" And we're like, "No, we're eighth grade." And he'll look at us and blink like he just noticed us, and go, "Oh, right."

You probably think I'm exaggerating, but I'm not. He's a good teacher, but his brain works kind of backward. Unless something happened two hundred years ago, he can't remember it.

I never had a class with Miss Rector, but a lot of kids like her. She's pretty, for a teacher, and she's smart. I was glad she was one of the teachers in charge of the Washington trip, because if Mr. Barto was in charge all by himself we'd have probably ended up in Brazil. Although looking back on it, that might have been better.

The chaperones were six moms and two dads, and the most important thing about them was, none of them was *my* mom or dad. I mean, I love my mom and dad, most of the time, but the older I get, the more I like to love them from a distance, if you know what I mean.

The class trip left early in the morning from the Miami airport. My parents dropped me off. My dad gave me some money and told me to spend it wisely, referring to the time in fourth grade when my class went to the Seaquarium and my dad gave me five dollars and I used it to buy five bags of Cheez-Its from a vending machine and I ate them all and on the way back to school I threw up orange glop all over the bus. My mom hugged me really hard and told me she loved me very much, and she was going to miss me, and if I did anything stupid in Washington she would kill me.

When the parents were gone Mr. Barto gathered all the kids and chaperones together for a little speech. He told us that it was a privilege for us to be on this trip to Washington and he expected us to be on our very best behavior as ambassadors representing Culver Middle School. That was when Cameron Frank farted. He's one of those kids who can fart whenever he wants to. His insides must be like 75 percent gas. Sometimes I think he could actually explode.

A bunch of kids laughed, and Mr. Barto glared at us and said that if we thought he was going to tolerate those kind of shenanigans—he actually said "shenanigans"—we were sadly mistaken, and he would not hesitate to send trouble-makers home, and did he make himself clear?

Everybody was quiet for about ten seconds while Mr. Barto looked around at us with a look that I guess was supposed to be scary. Then Cameron Frank farted again.

This time everybody laughed. Even the chaperones were trying not to crack up. Mr. Barto said a few more strict things, but I think he realized he was losing us, so he clapped his hands and said, "All right, let's go!" He started marching off, wearing his humongous backpack, like he was a general leading us into battle, except he was going the wrong direction. Miss Rector had to catch him and aim him the right way.

That was how we started our class trip.

We went through security and walked to the gate. I was technically walking with Matt Diaz and some other kids who are my friends, but I was trying to walk near Suzana Delgado.

I really, really like Suzana Delgado, who is the most beautiful girl in the eighth grade and probably the world. She has like 183 million Instagram followers. She's also really smart and funny and pretty nice for somebody that beautiful. Basically she's perfect, except for her height, which is: tall. Or at least taller than me. I'm kind of short. Okay, I'm not "kind of" short. I'm short. My mom claims everybody in our family started out short and I'll wind up normal, but that doesn't do me any good now.

The thing I wanted to do, more than anything else in the world, was to date Suzana Delgado. But I couldn't ask her. Not because she was tall, but because she was dating Jean-Philippe Dumas, better known as J.P., who's in the French program. He's also tall, even taller than Suzana. Sometimes I look at him, standing around being tall without even trying, and I want to kill him, except he could definitely beat me up.

My plan was to wait for J.P. and Suzana to break up, and

then see if she would date me. The problem was, they were like a permanent couple. When we went on the class trip, they'd been dating for nearly five weeks, which I think was a Culver Middle School record. But I still tried to talk to Suzana or text her whenever I could think of a reason.

Like, we were in the same math class, so every school night I'd text her to ask what the math homework was. The truth was, I already knew the math homework, and pretty soon she figured that out. But she went along with it, and it turned into kind of a joke, her making up funny answers. Like she'd say the math homework was to figure out the square root of a hamster, stuff like that. Sometimes we'd even make jokes about it in school, talking in person. I definitely think she liked me. But she was still dating J.P. And he was still tall.

So anyway, we got to our gate and stood around for a while, me standing near Suzana but not actually saying anything to her. When it was time to get on the plane, Mr. Barto told us we all had to go straight to our assigned seats, which we all did, except for Mr. Barto, who went straight to the completely wrong seat and had to be steered to the right one by Miss Rector.

I was in a middle seat next to Matt Diaz, who had a window seat on the left side of the plane. On my other side, unfortunately, was Cameron "Gas Attack" Frank. Suzana was two rows behind me with two of her friends. In the row between us were an old lady and two guys, probably in their thirties. One of them was short, with really long stringy hair that looked like seaweed, wearing sunglasses and a backpack and purple Crocs, which you don't usually see on a grown man. He had the window seat behind Matt. The other one was very big and very bald. He was wearing a black T-shirt, and he had huge arms with some kind of snakes tattooed on them. He was carrying a long black duffel bag, which he spent like five minutes trying to stuff into the overhead luggage space, holding up all the people trying to get to their seats. Finally one of the flight attendants, who was eighty jillion years old and probably was a flight attendant for the Wright brothers, came back and told the bald guy he would have to check the bag.

"No!" he said, like really angry. "It will fit!" He had some kind of accent, but not Spanish. He pushed the bag really hard and got it to go in. The flight attendant gave him a look, but didn't say anything. He looked like a guy you didn't want to get any more upset than he already was.

Which is exactly what my friend Matt, who I believe I already mentioned can be an idiot, proceeded to do. He pointed up at the luggage compartment and said—too loud, as usual—"What do you think he has in that bag? A missile?"

The big guy heard this. He looked down at Matt like he was about to pick him up by the neck and stuff him into the overhead space, which this guy was definitely big enough to do. The shorter guy with the sunglasses said something to him, and he sat down.

"Jeez," said Matt, still too loud. "Maybe it *is* a missile."

"Will you shut *up*?" I said, but it was too late: We looked back, and the big guy was leaning forward, his head almost in our row, glaring at Matt, for like ten seconds, just leaning over us and *staring*. He was really close, and he looked a little crazy, and I'll be honest: I was scared. Then the little guy said something again, and the big guy sat back. Matt and I looked at each other, like *whoa*, but even Matt wasn't stupid enough to say anything else.

When the plane was loaded the same flight attendant came down the aisle checking things, and she told the little guy he couldn't hold his backpack in his lap.

He said, "I need to hold it."

"I'm sorry, sir," she said, not sounding sorry. "You can't hold it during takeoff or landing."

"Is very important."

"You can hold it after we take off. Right now it has to go in the overhead." She reached for the backpack.

"No!" said the little guy, pulling it away.

"All right," she said, "then you'll have to put it under the seat in front of you."

"I am not comfortable doing that."

"*Sir,*" said the flight attendant, "you can*not* have that in your lap. Either you stow it now, or you'll have to get off the plane."

This time the big guy said something quietly to the little guy, in what I think was a foreign language. The little guy sighed and stuck the backpack under the seat in front of him, which was the seat that Matt was sitting in. The flight attendant gave the little guy a look and walked away.

Matt leaned over to me. "What do you think's in the backpack?" he said—whispering, fortunately.

"How would I know?" I said.

"You think it's a bomb?"

"No!"

"Why not?"

"Because, moron, he had to go through security."

"Well, then what is it? Why's he acting so weird? Him and his friend with the missile . . ."

"It's not a missile!" I said, too loud—that's the kind of thing Matt makes you do—and all of a sudden I realized the big guy was leaning forward and glaring at us again, so I shut up. We stayed quiet during the safety lecture where they show you how to fasten your seat belt and tell you that your seat cushion floats, which I'm sure would be really helpful if the plane actually crashed into the ocean at five hundred miles an hour.

I noticed that after we took off, the little guy immediately reached down and got the backpack out from under Matt's seat. But then I stopped thinking about him and started trying to figure out how to talk to Suzana, two rows behind. My idea was to pretend I had to go to the bathroom, and then, when I walked past her, I would say some funny thing that would make her laugh, and we would start having a conversation, with me standing in the aisle, which was good because I would be standing and she would be sitting down so I'd be taller.

This seemed like a solid plan, except for one thing: I didn't have anything funny to say. I spent the first half hour of the flight trying to think of jokes, which wasn't easy because Matt kept whispering to me about the guys behind us, who he was convinced were terrorists planning to blow up the plane.

Finally I came up with a joke: I'd walk by, and I'd say to Suzana, casually, like I just thought of it, "Do you know where the emergency exit is?" And she'd say something like, "Why are you looking for the emergency exit?" And I'd say, "Because I'm sitting next to Cameron Frank, and I need some fresh air!"

I'm not saying this was hilarious. I'm saying this was the best I could do under the circumstances. I was going over my lines in my head ("Do you know where the emergency exit is?"), rehearsing for my big moment. Meanwhile Matt kept sneaking peeks back at the weird two guys behind us and whispering reports to me.

"They're looking at something," he said.

"So what?" I said.

"We need to find out what it is," he said.

"No we don't," I said.

Anyway, we finally got to the altitude where you can walk around, so I got up and started toward the back of the plane. I noticed out of the side of my eye that the two weird guys behind us actually *were* looking at something, kind of hunched over it so you couldn't see what it was. But I was focused on Suzana. I was so focused on Suzana that I didn't see that the man in the seat right across the aisle had his leg sticking out.

What happened next was the kind of horrible embarrassing failure that your brain memorizes every single detail of so it can torture you by playing it in your head over and over and over for the rest of your life. This is how it went:

> **ME** (*to Suzana, pretending I am just thinking this up as I pass by*): Hey, do you know where th— *WHAM* (*sound of me tripping and falling on my face in the aisle*).
> **SUZANA:** Ohmigod! Wyatt! Are you okay?

ME *(getting up, trying to look like nothing happened)*: I'm fine! I'm fine!

SUZANA: Are you sure?

ME *(thinking for some moronic reason that I should still do my moronic rehearsed joke)*: I was just wondering if you knew where the emergency exit was.

EIGHTY-JILLION-YEAR-OLD FLIGHT ATTENDANT *(coming down the aisle to see why I fell down and not looking happy)*: What's going on here?

ME: Nothing. I fell down.

SUZANA: Why do you need the emergency exit?

EIGHTY-JILLION-YEAR-OLD FLIGHT ATTENDANT: What about the emergency exit?

ME: Nothing!

SUZANA: You just asked me where the emergency exit is.

ME *(reaching new heights of being a moron)*: I did?

SUZANA: Yes, you did.

EIGHTY-JILLION-YEAR-OLD FLIGHT ATTENDANT *(to me)*: Do you not understand that the emergency exits are an important safety feature of this aircraft, and it's a very serious matter to tamper with them in any way?

ME: No.

EIGHTY-JILLION-YEAR-OLD FLIGHT ATTENDANT: No?

ME: Yes! I mean, yes, I understand. I wasn't really . . . I was just . . . There's this kid who farts. . . .

EIGHTY-JILLION-YEAR-OLD FLIGHT ATTENDANT:
What?

MR. BARTO (*coming down the aisle from his seat*)**:** Is
something wrong?

EIGHTY-JILLION-YEAR-OLD FLIGHT ATTENDANT: This
young man seems to think there's something amusing
about the emergency exits.

MR. BARTO: Wyatt, do you think there's something
amusing about the emergency exits?

ME: No. I was—

EIGHTY-JILLION-YEAR-OLD FLIGHT ATTENDANT: He also
said something about farts.

MR. BARTO: What about farts, Wyatt?

ME: No! I was only . . . nothing. Never mind.

MR. BARTO: Wyatt, I want you to return to your seat *right
now*, and if you don't want to be sent home from this
trip, there had better be no more of this behavior, am I
clear?

ME: Yes.

I went back to my seat. Behind me I could hear Suzana
and her friends giggling. Now I really did wish I could jump
out the emergency exit.

"What was *that* all about?" said Matt.

"Shut up," I said.

"Listen," he said, not shutting up, "the guys behind us were watching you."

"Great."

"No, *listen*. While they were watching you, I got a look at what they were looking at."

"Good for you."

"And get this. They're looking at aerial photographs."

"So?"

"They're aerial photographs of the *White House*."

I looked at him. "Are you sure?"

He nodded twice really fast, up-down-up-down, and whispered, "Aerial photographs *of the White House*."

I thought about that for a couple of seconds. "There could be a simple explanation," I said.

"Like what?"

"Like, I dunno, they're tourists, and they'll be walking around the White House area, and they want to see what's around there, from the air." Even while I was saying this, it sounded stupid.

Matt shook his head. "Tourists use *maps*. Not aerial photographs."

I ducked down and snuck a peek between Matt's and my seatbacks at the weird guys behind us. They were looking at something, and they were definitely hunching over it like they didn't want anybody walking past in the aisle to see. But from my angle, I got a quick glimpse. And Matt was right: It was a photo of the White House, taken from the air. I looked back at Matt. He raised his eyebrows.

"See?" he said.

"What do you think they're doing?"

"Add it up," he said. "There's two weird guys, both carrying things that they're acting all weird about, right?"

"Right."

"And now they're looking at an aerial photograph of the White House, right?"

"Right."

"Now think about it: What does this airplane practically fly *right over* when we get to Washington?"

I thought about it. I went to Washington with my family in fourth grade, and I remembered that when the plane was landing, it flew over the Potomac River, and my dad was pointing to famous stuff out the left-side window, really close—the Washington Monument, the Lincoln Memorial . . . and the White House.

"Oh, man," I said.

"Yeah," said Matt. "And you laughed when I said they had a missile."

"But they can't have a missile. They got through airport security."

Matt snorted. "Did you *see* those airport security people?

I think you could drive a tank past them, as long as it didn't contain any liquids."

"No, seriously, there's no way they could—"

"Okay, okay, say it's not a missile. Maybe it's some other kind of weapon, something that has two pieces, and it's only dangerous if you put them together. One piece is in the big guy's black bag up there, and the other's in the weird little dude's backpack. When we get near Washington, they put the pieces together and it forms some kind of new thing that does something bad."

"Like what?"

"Like blow up the plane. Or it's some kind of high-tech gun, or a thing they can use to smash through the cockpit door. I don't know what it is. But it's *something*."

I thought about it some more. Matt can be an idiot, but he's not a *complete* idiot.

I said, "So what should we do?"

"Maybe we should tell the flight attendant."

I looked toward the front of the plane. The mean eighty-jillion-year-old flight attendant was glaring around the cabin like she was about to cast a spell and turn everybody into a frog. I imagined what it would be like to go up to her and tell her that we thought the two guys behind us were terrorists, based on . . . based on not a whole lot, really.

"Why don't you tell her?" I said.

"*I'm* not gonna tell her," said Matt. "Why don't you tell her?"

"She already hates me," I said.

"I think she hates everybody," said Matt.

"Okay," I said. "We won't say anything now. But we'll watch them. If they do anything weird, especially when we're getting near the White House, we'll do something."

"Like what?"

"Like yell. Or something."

"That's our plan? We yell? Or something?"

"Do you have a better plan?"

"No."

"Then that's our plan."

For the next hour or so we just sat there feeling nervous. I was so nervous I didn't even think about Suzana. Every now and then we snuck a peek back between the seats at the weird guys. They had put away the photograph and mostly talked in low voices. The little guy kept the backpack on his lap.

Then the pilot announced that we were beginning our descent into Washington. He said there was turbulence and it was going to be "a little bumpy" and everybody should make sure their seat belts were fastened. They told us to turn off our laptop computers and put everything away. Matt and I peeked back and saw that the weird little guy still had his backpack in his lap. The eighty-jillion-year-old flight attendant came by and stopped next to him.

"Sir," she said. "You have to put that away."

"I would prefer to hold it," he said.

"Sir," she said, and you could tell she was about to lose it, *"you have to put it away."*

The little guy looked like he was about to say something. But then he put it away. The backpack was now right under Matt's seat.

We could feel the plane descending, then turning. We were over the Potomac River now. Matt and I were sneaking a lot of peeks back. The two weird guys were staring out the window. The air started getting bumpy. *Really* bumpy. Stuff on the plane was rattling and people were making nervous sounds. The plane was really low now. I could see buildings out the left-side window. I peeked back. The two weird guys were glued to the window, the big guy leaning over into the little guy's seat, the two of them staring out.

"We're coming up on the White House," said Matt.

Right then the plane bumped hard. It felt like we slammed into an elephant in midair. Some people screamed. I was really scared. There was another huge bump and the whole plane lurched sideways. More screams.

Suddenly Matt grabbed my arm and said, "He's getting the backpack!" I looked back and saw that the little weird guy was leaning down toward the storage area under Matt's seat.

"We gotta stop him!" said Matt.

I was going to ask him how, but before I could say anything he turned around and slid down off his seat onto the floor, into the foot space.

"What are you *doing*?" I said, but then I saw. He was reaching under his seat and grabbing the guy's backpack, trying to pull it through the opening under his seat.

"No!" shouted the little weird guy, from behind us. "Let go of that! Let go!"

Now there was a tug-of-war going on, with Matt trying to pull the backpack forward and the little weird guy trying to pull it back. The little weird guy kept yelling at Matt to let go, but he wouldn't. The big weird guy leaned forward over the seat, also yelling at Matt and trying to grab him, but he had his seat belt on, so Matt was too low for him to reach. People around us saw what was happening, but the plane was still bumping and shaking pretty hard, so most of the passengers were too busy being nervous to notice. Outside the window I could see the land getting closer, and then *whump* the plane touched down hard, bounced, and then stayed down. Some people cheered. Meanwhile Matt and the little weird guy were still fighting their tug-of-war, the little guy still shouting at Matt to let go of the backpack. The big weird guy was standing up now, leaning over into our row.

"Sir! Sit down!" This was the eighty-jillion-year-old flight attendant shouting over the P.A. system. The big guy sat down, but he kept trying to reach Matt. The plane was slowing down. More people were looking at our row, trying to see what the yelling was about. The eighty-jillion-year-old flight attendant was coming down the aisle toward us, looking very unhappy.

"Got it!" said Matt, pulling the backpack all the way through the seat.

"GIVE IT TO ME!" shouted the little guy, practically diving over the seat, grabbing at Matt.

Matt was leaning over the backpack, protecting it with his body. I could see he was unzipping one of the side pockets. Now both the big guy and the little guy were leaning over him. The big guy grabbed him under his arms and started lifting him, pulling him right up through the seat belt.

"Wyatt, here!" said Matt. He shoved the backpack at me, and without really thinking about it, I took it. Which meant I was holding it when the flight attendant got to our row. The plane had just rolled to a stop, and pretty much everybody was now looking in our direction.

"What's going on here?" said the flight attendant. "Why are you holding that boy?"

The big guy let go of Matt, who plopped back down into his seat.

"That boy has my property!" shouted the little guy, pointing at me.

So now everybody on the plane was looking at me. Not Matt. Me.

"Is that his backpack?" said the flight attendant.

"Um," I said. Which I admit was not a brilliant statement, but it was definitely smarter than what Matt said, which was, quote: "It has a bomb in it!"

You can imagine what a big hit *that* was, on a crowded airplane. People started screaming and trying to get away, but we were still taxiing on the runway, so the doors were closed, and there was nowhere to go.

"QUIET!" shouted a deep voice, so loud that people actually got pretty quiet. "Everybody back in your seats *now*."

The deep voice belonged to a wide man in jeans and a sweater who was coming down the aisle from first class. People were getting out of his way and sitting back down.

"I'm a Federal Air Marshal," the wide man said. "What's going on here?"

The flight attendant pointed to me and said, "He says he has a bomb."

This was not really true, but before I could point that out, the marshal said to me, "What's your name, son?"

"Wyatt Palmer."

"What's in that backpack?"

"I don't know."

"Then why'd you say it was a bomb?"

"I didn't."

"Then who did?"

"I did," said Matt.

The wide man looked at Matt.

"And you are?"

"Matthew Diaz."

"Okay, why did *you* say it was a bomb?"

Matt pointed at the two weird guys behind us and said, "It belongs to them and they were acting weird."

"How were they acting weird?"

"They were looking at aerial photos of the White House."

The marshal looked at the two guys and said, "Is that true?"

The big guy said, "Yes." He held up a book. On the cover was an aerial photo of the Capitol. The book was titled *Washington from the Air.* "We are tourists," said the big guy. "We are first time coming to city of Washington, so we are reading this book."

The marshal looked at Matt. "So that's why you thought they had a bomb?"

"Not just that!" said Matt. He pointed at the little guy. "When the plane was coming over the White House, he was reaching for his backpack!"

The marshal looked at the little guy and said, "Were you reaching for the backpack?"

"No," said the little guy. "I was reaching for this." He held up a barf bag. It looked full.

"Ew," said Suzana Delgado.

The marshal looked at me and said, "Give me the backpack." I gave it to him. He looked at the little guy and said, "Do you mind if I look inside?"

I thought the little guy hesitated just a tenth of a second before he said, "No, is fine."

The marshal unzipped the backpack and looked inside. He looked up at the little guy and said, "Mind if I take it out?"

The little guy nodded. "Of course," he said. "But please be careful."

The marshal set the backpack down on a seat, reached inside, and pulled out . . .

A dragon's head.

It was made out of some lightweight material and painted a million colors. It had big buggy eyes and an open mouth filled with long sharp fangy-looking teeth.

The marshal held it up and looked at it. "Nice," he said.

"Thank you," said the little guy. "I made it. I am artist. I make traditional folk art from my country."

"And what country is that?"

"Gadakistan. Is near—"

"I know where it is." The marshal put the dragon head back into the backpack and handed it to the little guy. He looked at Matt and me. It wasn't a friendly look.

"Listen," said Matt. "I still think . . ."

I grabbed his arm. "Shut up," I said.

"But there's—"

"Just for once shut *up*, okay?"

The plane was at the gate now, and the front door was opening. People were standing and getting their stuff down from the overhead storage. I reached down to get my backpack, hoping that somehow all this would just go away. But . . .

"Hold it," said the marshal, putting his hand on my shoulder. "You boys are staying right here."

Matt and I sat in our seats while everybody else got off the plane, except Mr. Barto, who stood with his arms folded, staring at us. The worst was when other kids went past us. Some of them were laughing. Suzana looked at me and just shook her head.

The two weird guys took their time getting ready to leave,

so they were almost the last ones off. The big guy got his long black bag down from the overhead, and the two of them headed for the front of the plane. When they got there, the little one turned and looked back. He made sure the marshal wasn't looking his way. Then he looked straight at me and Matt, held up his backpack, and smiled at us.

A really creepy smile.

CHAPTER 2

The only good part about what happened next was that the Federal Marshal decided not to arrest me and Matt. He said he seriously considered it, but in the end he decided to let us off with just a lecture on the general theme that we were a pair of idiots.

The worst part was when I had to call my parents from the airport and tell them that Mr. Barto was maybe going to send me and Matt home from Washington. I didn't really need my phone after I said that, because I could have heard my mother—did I mention that she's Cuban?—yelling all the way from Miami. Basically she said she was going to kill me *and* ground me *and* take away my Xbox for the next three hundred years. Which didn't make any sense, but it was not a good time to point that out to my mom.

After that Matt and I had to listen to another lecture, this one from Mr. Barto, which he delivered to us next to the bus at the airport with the entire class trip sitting on the bus watching and making faces. Mr. Barto said he was extremely disappointed in us because we were ambassadors for Culver Middle School and it was a privilege to be on this trip and if we pulled one more stupid stunt he was going to blah blah blah.

In the end he said we could stay on the trip. He claimed this was because he was a forgiving man, but I think mainly he was a man who didn't want to deal with trying to get us home.

I was just glad I wouldn't have to face my mom yet.

When Matt and I finally got on the bus the only seat left was (of course) right behind Cameron Frank, whose general area smelled like a Porta Potti in July. And of course Suzana was sitting far away with the other hot girls, near Jean-Philippe. But at least we were on the bus, instead of on a plane home. I was starting to feel less bad, maybe even almost a little good.

That feeling lasted about thirty seconds.

I didn't see them coming. The bus driver had just closed

the door. I was looking forward when Matt, who was sitting next to the window, grabbed my arm.

"Uh-oh," he said.

"What?"

He pointed out the window. I almost yelped when I saw them.

The two weird guys from the plane. Running toward our bus. Looking very unhappy.

Their eyes were scanning the windows, and it wasn't hard to figure out who they were looking for. I was about to tell Matt to duck, but it was too late: The little guy saw us. He ran straight to our window. He was holding up his backpack and pointing to it and yelling something at us. The big guy was right behind him. They looked *really* mad.

"What do they want?" I said.

Matt didn't say anything.

Just then the bus started moving. This totally freaked out the two guys. They started running toward the front, shouting, but the bus was pulling away into the airport traffic. The weird guys started to chase us, but they ran into a cop directing traffic. We saw him block their way, holding up his hands for them to stop. They were arguing with him and pointing at us. The last thing I saw before we got out of sight was the little guy's face. He looked really, really, *really* mad.

Mr. Barto and Miss Rector, at the front of the bus, missed

all of this. The kids around us saw it, and they were asking us what was going on. I said I didn't know, that maybe the guys were still mad about what happened on the plane.

Matt still didn't say anything. Which, if you know anything about Matt, is very unusual. Suddenly I had a bad feeling.

"Wait a minute," I said to Matt, keeping it quiet. "*You* know what that was about, don't you."

"Um, maybe."

I grabbed his arm. "What? *What?*"

"Okay! Let go!" He yanked his arm away. He looked around to make sure nobody was looking our way, then reached into his pocket and pulled something out. He kept it low and showed it to me. It was some kind of electronic thing, a greenish-brown box with a little Plexiglas dome on the top and some switches and buttons on the side.

"Where'd you get that?" I said, even though I pretty much knew.

"From the weird guy's backpack. It was in the outside pocket."

"Why'd you take it?"

"I thought it was maybe a detonator. I thought he was gonna blow something up with it."

"Blow up *what?* His dragon head?"

"I didn't know he had a dragon head in there."

I looked at the box. "Why didn't you tell the marshal about it?"

"I was gonna. But you told me to shut up. Then I decided it was better to just keep quiet about it. I didn't want to get in any more trouble."

We both looked at the box for a few seconds.

"Maybe I should just throw it away," he said.

I shook my head. "He seemed really upset about losing it. It might be valuable. We should give it back."

"How?"

"I dunno."

"How would we even find those guys?"

"I dunno."

"Do we even *want* to find those guys?"

I looked out the window. The bus was out of the airport now, on a highway. I thought about the two weird guys back there, probably still arguing with the cop. I pictured the little guy's face, the way he looked at us as the bus pulled away.

"Not really," I said. "I hope we never see those guys again."

CHAPTER 3

retty soon we crossed a bridge into Washington. Up ahead we could see the Capitol and a bunch of other Washington-y stuff. Mr. Barto got on the bus P.A. microphone and started pointing out historic things, but since he's Mr. Barto he kept getting them wrong. Like he'd say, "Over here to the left you can see the Lincoln Memorial," and Miss Rector would whisper something to him, and he'd say, "I mean the Jefferson Memorial."

Our hotel was a big grayish building called the Warren G. Harding Hotel. It was really old. I think it was the official hotel of every Washington class trip since the Civil War.

The lobby had saggy sofas that looked like some kind of farm animals gave birth on them. One kid claimed he saw a rat heading into the coffee shop. But nobody really cared, because we were in a hotel and our parents weren't.

Mr. Barto gathered us all together to tell us he was expecting everybody to behave in a manner blah blah blah. Meanwhile Miss Rector got the room key cards from the guy at the front desk and handed them out. I was in room 313 with three roommates: Matt, Cameron (of course), and a kid named Victor Lopez, who was new to Culver, so he didn't have a lot of friends, which is why he ended up with us. He was in my science class and didn't say much, but he seemed pretty smart.

We got into an elevator that made clunking noises and moved really slow, like it was tired of being an elevator and wanted to retire and just be a closet or something. We got off on the third floor and found room 313, which smelled like a small animal once died in it and they never found the body. It had a rattling air conditioner and an old boxy TV that probably ran on coal. We unpacked our suitcases and put our stuff away. Matt put the detonator, or whatever it was, under his clothes in his drawer.

We decided that, between the room smell and Cameron, we needed to open the window, which was hard because it was kind of painted shut. When Matt and I finally shoved it open I leaned out and saw that our room was right over the roof above the hotel front driveway. While I was leaning out I heard a voice say "Hello," which surprised me so much that I jerked my head straight up and banged it on the window frame. The voice giggled, and I looked to my right and saw it was Suzana leaning out of the next window over. She gave me a smile that made my stomach jump.

"Does your room smell as bad as ours?" she said.

"Worse," I said. "We have Cameron in here. I'm thinking of sleeping with my head out the window."

She laughed—I *really* like it when I make her laugh—then said, "So what was that about back there? In the plane?"

I shook my head. "Those two weird guys . . . You saw them, right?"

"Yeah."

"Well, I let Matt convince me they were trying to blow up the White House."

"On the plane? Blow it up how?"

"With a missile. Or something."

She blinked. "A missile?"

"I know it sounds stupid. It *is* stupid. I can't believe he got me to take it seriously. I think Matt has this ability to lower the IQ of everybody around him. It's like a superpower."

Suzana laughed again. Suddenly this was seeming like not such a totally horrible class trip.

So of course Matt had to ruin everything.

He stuck his head out next to mine and said, "Hey, Suzana! You know Wyatt loves you, right?"

"Shut up, idiot," I said, trying to push him back inside.

"Wait for him, Suzana!" shouted Matt. "He'll get taller someday!"

"Shut UP," I said, still pushing.

"Maybe not this year, Suzana!" shouted Matt. "Maybe not for many years! But some day, when you're seventy, you might start shrinking, and Wyatt could catch up to you! Wait for him!"

I shoved him really hard. The two of us stumbled back into the room and fell on the floor, and he finally stopped yelling, because he was laughing too hard to breathe. I got back up and stuck my head out the window.

Suzana was gone. I turned around and looked down at Matt.

"You are *such* an idiot."

"Maybe," he said, catching his breath. "But at least I don't think Suzana Delgado might actually like me."

"She does like me."

"As a *friend*. Which is also how she likes her dog. And which is not how she likes J.P."

I didn't have an answer for that, since it was true.

Victor was standing by the door, watching us with a

frowny expression, like he was looking through a microscope and we were some kind of fungus cells.

"We're supposed to be in the lobby," he said. "For the bus tour."

So we got into the sad old elevator and clunked down to the lobby and stood around in clots waiting for the bus. I didn't even want to look in the direction of the Hot Girl clot because I was so embarrassed about what Matt yelled out the window to Suzana. But I glanced that way and just for a second she looked at me and smiled and I kind of smiled back and then looked away, trying to look casual, like I had other things on my mind besides her, except of course I didn't and my face was probably the same color as a stop sign.

How do girls *do* this?

The bus came and we got on for our tour and I was happy about two things:

1. I didn't get stuck next to Cameron.

2. Instead of Mr. Barto, we had an actual professional tour guide. His name was Gene Weingarten. You know those joke disguise glasses that make you look like Groucho Marx, with the big nose and the huge bushy black eyebrows and the bushy black mustache? Well, Gene—he said we should call him Gene—looked exactly like that, except he wasn't wearing disguise glasses. That was his regular look. But he

was a way better guide than Mr. Barto, because he seemed to actually know what he was pointing to.

We drove around Washington looking at famous things, with Gene explaining what they were and Mr. Barto grabbing the microphone about every three seconds to tell us that if we didn't pay attention he was going to take away everybody's phones and blah blah blah. Some of the things were pretty cool to see, like the Capitol. Some of the things were basically just big buildings where, according to Mr. Weingarten, something historic happened inside, but from the outside to be honest they just looked like buildings.

The bus parked near the Washington Monument and we all got out and sat on the grass and Miss Rector handed out box lunches with sandwiches containing some kind of slimy meat that looked a cross between a really sick chicken and a really pale ham. Chickham. I ate the potato chips and gave my sandwich to Cameron, who ate it in like three bites, which probably explains the way his digestive system works.

After lunch we had a few minutes of free time. A bunch of boys, including Matt and me, went to this kind of dumpy store that sold supposedly funny T-shirts and joke items and patriotic souvenirs of Washington made in China. Matt bought a cigarette lighter that looked like a gun. You pulled the trigger and the flame appeared at the end. I bought a T-shirt that said U.S. SECRET SERVICE on the front, although

44

I imagine a real Secret Service agent would never wear it because then they wouldn't be very secret.

After that Gene took us on a walking tour to the World War II Memorial, the Korean War Memorial, the Lincoln Memorial, the Martin Luther King Jr. Memorial, and the Vietnam Memorial, which is a lot of memorials and a lot of walking, plus it was a warm day, not Miami warm, but warm. Mr. Barto, who was carrying that giant backpack he always had on, looked like he was going to pass out. After those monuments we stood in line to go up in the Washington Monument, which was a long wait but a pretty great view from the top.

When we came out there were a bunch of guys flying kites near the monument. Gene told us they were practicing for a huge kite festival that was going to happen in a few days. Some of the kites had really cool designs, like a fish, or a centipede, or a giant spider, or just a lot of weird shapes. Sometimes you couldn't even imagine how they could fly, but they did. Some of the kites were huge. One of them actually lifted the guy holding it off the ground for a few seconds before he could get control of it.

From there we walked to the White House, and I have to say it was pretty amazing to say we were at the White House, even though we weren't actually going in, just walking along the big iron fence outside it.

Gene told us that for a long time, there was no security at the White House. Regular people could just walk in off the street and see, like, Abraham Lincoln. But now there was tons of security—bulletproof glass, motion sensors above and below the ground, lasers, Secret Service guys everywhere, snipers on the roof, even missiles in case they had to shoot down an airplane.

"Every now and then somebody climbs the fence, but they usually catch the person quickly," Gene said. We asked what happens to those people.

"You don't want to know," he said.

We walked along the gate on the Pennsylvania Avenue side and took a bunch of pictures of ourselves smiling like morons with the White House in the background, which is also what about ninety million other tourists were doing. After a while Miss Rector said we had to get back to the bus and started herding us. We reached a corner and turned down a street that ran alongside the White House grounds near where our bus was parked. We were kind of flowing along in a big river of tourists, and I was looking forward to getting to the bus and sitting down after all that walking. That was all I was thinking about.

Until I saw a bald head.

It was up ahead, bobbing along in the tourist river, sticking out over the rest of the heads.

The bald head of a big guy.

I sped up, got a little closer, a little better look.

The bald guy was wearing a black T-shirt.

I did *not* want it to be the guy from the plane. I tried to convince myself that it probably wasn't. I mean, Washington was a big city full of people. There was probably more than one big bald guy wearing a black T-shirt. This is what I told myself.

But I wanted to make sure. I started walking faster. I got past a bunch of people, so I was maybe ten yards behind the bald guy. That's when I saw the snakes tattooed on his arms. And the weird little guy walking next to him.

I stopped so fast that the person behind me bumped into me, which was okay because it was Matt.

"Hey!" he said.

"Problem," I said.

"What?"

I grabbed his arm and tugged him to the side, so he could see past the people in front of us. I pointed ahead.

"Oh, man," he said.

"Yeah."

"We can't let them see us."

"Duh."

We slowed down and let more people go past. We were the last ones in our group now, trailing behind everybody. I

47

could still see the bald guy's head up ahead. He was a really big guy. We kept as far back as we could and still see our class group. The White House was on our right now. At the end of the block the bald guy and the little guy peeled off and went to the right, toward the gate where people were lined up for the White House tour. The two guys walked a few yards, then stopped. Which meant we were going to walk right past where they were standing.

"Uh-oh," said Matt.

"Just keep walking."

At that moment the two guys weren't looking our way. They were staring at the White House. The big guy pointed at the fence and said something, and the little guy nodded. They moved closer to the fence, studying it.

Matt and I were almost even with them now. We started walking faster.

We were even with them now.

The little guy's head started to turn.

I looked away and walked even faster.

"Hey!"

The little guy had seen us. I looked: They were both coming after us.

Looking back, I still don't know whether Matt and I handled it right. The smartest thing might have been to run to the front of the group and get next to Mr. Barto, Miss

Rector, and Gene. The two guys probably wouldn't have dared try to grab us right in front of grown-ups. On the other hand, they might have told the grown-ups about Matt taking the detonator (or whatever it was) from the little guy's backpack, and we might have gotten in even more trouble and been sent home.

The thing is, when it happened, there wasn't a lot of time to think. There was just these two scary weird guys coming after us looking mad.

So we ran.

We took off to the left, away from the White House, across the street, which was not brilliant because there were cars coming, but we made it to the other side okay. I looked back and saw that the two guys were waiting for a break in traffic to get across. I also saw that the rest of our class group had reached the end of the block and was heading to where the bus was parked. Nobody had seen Matt and me take off; we were on our own.

And now the weird guys were crossing the street.

Matt and I ran down a side street, still heading away from the White House. We got to an intersection. We looked back and saw the weird guys coming. I noticed two things, one bad and one good. The bad one was, they looked extremely mad. Like if they caught us, they would not only kill us, but also eat us.

The good news was, they were not fast runners.

We turned right and started running again. Our plan was to circle around and get back to where the bus was parked. We ran to the end of the street and turned right again. Now we were headed back toward the White House. We crossed another street and turned left. Up ahead we could see a line of parked buses. I was praying one of them would be ours.

I looked back. The weird guys were a long ways back now.

"That's our bus," said Matt, pointing.

We sprinted to the bus. Everybody was already on it except Mr. Barto, who was standing next to the doorway staring at us with his arms crossed. I could tell he was about to give us a stern lecture about how he had given us one more chance to shape up and now blah blah blah. I was pretty sure our class trip was over.

But every now and then, Matt turns out not to be a complete idiot, and this was one of those times. Before Mr. Barto could say a word, he said, "I had to go to the bathroom."

"What?" said Mr. Barto.

"Diarrhea," said Matt. "It was really bad. REALLY bad. I had to go behind a tree." He waved in the general direction of the White House. "I didn't have any toilet paper, so Wyatt had to ask people if they had any Kleenex."

I nodded. The loyal Kleenex-getting friend. Mr. Barto

was frowning, trying to process this. I snuck a glance behind us. I didn't see the weird guys.

"But nobody had any Kleenex," said Matt, getting into the dramatic story of him having imaginary diarrhea. "But this one lady had a *People* magazine, so Matt brought me that and I tore out some pages and used that. It was a feature on One Direction. You know them, Mr. Barto? One Direction? It's like this boy band. There's five of them, so that was like five pages. But like I said this was a *really* messy situation, so I had to tear out another article, which was about this girl with no legs who becomes a baton twirler and tries out for her high school—"

"Diaz!" shouted Mr. Barto.

"What?"

"Shut up and get on the bus."

Matt gave me a look. *Mission accomplished.*

"Hey!"

The shout came from behind us. Matt and I didn't have to look to see who it was. We quickly followed Mr. Barto onto the bus, and the driver, who'd been waiting for us, shut the door. We scurried to our seats as the bus started moving. I looked out the window, and there were the two weird guys, running after us. They were waving their arms and shouting, and their faces were bright red. They were too far away to catch us. I sat back in my seat and whooshed the air out of my lungs. My heart was pounding and I was covered in sweat. As far as I could tell, the rest of the kids on the bus hadn't seen the guys chasing us.

"Pretty fast thinking, huh?" said Matt. "Diarrhea? *People* magazine? One Direction?"

"Yeah, you're a genius. Except you're also the reason they're after us. Whatever that thing is you took, maybe you should just give it back to them."

"The detonator?"

"You don't know it's a detonator."

"It's *something*, Wyatt. They want it back *bad*. Which is why we shouldn't let them have it."

"Why should we care?"

"Think about it. On the plane they were looking at aerial photos of the White House."

"So? They said—"

"I know what they *said*. But they're weird guys, and I still say that was a weird thing for them to be doing. And it's really weird that they brought a detonator."

"You don't know it's a—"

"Just *listen*. And when we see them again, where are they? At the *White House*."

"So? *We* were at the White House, too."

"Right. But we were looking at the White House, because we're tourists. They were looking at the fence. You saw them."

I thought about it. They *had* seemed interested in the fence. "So what do you think they're doing?"

"Scouting."

"Scouting what?"

"I dunno. But maybe we should tell Mr. Barto."

"Tell him what? That the two guys we accused on the plane because they seemed weird still seem weird? And they want us to give them back something that belongs to them? Which you stole from their backpack?"

Matt thought about that. "It doesn't sound so good, does it?"

"It sounds like a way to get us sent home."

"So what do *you* think we should do?"

"Nothing."

"Nothing?"

"Look, either they're planning something bad, or they're not, right?"

"Right."

"So if they're *not*, and they're just weird guys, then doing nothing is the best thing, right?"

"Right."

"And if they *are* planning something bad, and that's why they want that thing you took, then they can't do whatever it is, because you have the thing, and they don't know where you are. Right?"

"I guess."

"So we don't have to do anything."

"But what if they keep looking for us?"

"How're they going to find us? In this whole giant city?"

Matt frowned, looking like he wasn't sure.

"They're way back there," I said, waving in the general direction of the back of the bus. "We're not gonna see them again." I hoped this was true.

Matt looked out the window. Finally he said, "Yeah, I guess not."

We both got quiet then. Gene was back on the microphone, telling us more historic stuff about Washington. Then Mr. Barto got on and told us the schedule for the evening. Then Miss Rector got on and told us the real schedule for the evening, because Mr. Barto had actually given us the schedule for the following evening. We were going to eat dinner at a restaurant and then go to a concert by a military band.

By the time we got back to the Warren G. Harding I was feeling pretty good, like everything really was going to be okay. That feeling lasted until we got off the bus in front of the hotel, which was when Matt grabbed my arm.

"What?" I said.

"That." He pointed at the bus.

"What?" I said again.

He went closer to the bus and pointed to writing painted on the side:

SHRODER TRANSPORTATION
NEED A BUS? CALL US!

Underneath there was a phone number.

"So what?" I said.

"So what if those guys call the bus company and find out where this bus went?"

"But how would they know which bus we . . ." I stopped, because I could already see the answer, painted on the side of the bus in big numbers: **147**.

"This is bad," said Matt.

"Okay," I said. "Let's say they call the bus company. They probably won't tell them anything."

"You don't know that."

I pulled out my phone. "Let's find out."

I dialed the bus company number. A lady's voice said, "Shroder Transportation."

"Hi," I said. "I'm . . . uh . . . I'm a student on a class trip here in Washington, and I'm . . . uh . . . trying to find my bus."

"You lost your bus?"

"Yeah, I got separated from the group. But I know the bus number. It's 147."

"Right now bus 147 is at the Harding Hotel." She sounded kind of annoyed.

"Um, thanks," I said.

"You people need to keep better track of that bus."

Suddenly I had a bad feeling in my stomach.

"What do you mean?" I said.

"I mean you're the second person to call about it. That's how I know off the top of my head where it is."

"Somebody else called about bus 147?"

"Maybe ten minutes ago."

"Who was it?"

"A man."

"A man?"

"Said he was a teacher."

I looked toward the hotel entrance and saw Mr. Barto and Miss Rector. They were the only Culver teachers on this trip. I started to ask the bus company lady another question. "Can you tell me—"

But she had hung up.

CHAPTER 4

"They're coming here," said Matt. "They're gonna come here looking for us."

We were back in our room, leaning out the window, talking quietly. Cameron and Victor were watching TV.

"They don't know what room we're in," I said.

"They can just wait for us in the lobby. Sooner or later they'll see us walking in or out."

We both stared out the window. A taxi pulled up in front of the hotel, with two people in the back. The door opened, and we both held our breath. But it was just two lady tourists. We both exhaled.

"Seriously," I said, "maybe we should just give that thing back to them."

Matt shook his head. "No. Those are not good guys. Whatever they want it for, it's probably bad."

"So maybe we should call the police."

He shook his head again. "You said it yourself. We really can't prove anything about them, except they're weird. We couldn't even prove that thing is theirs."

"So what do we do?"

"We keep the thing away from them, and we try to figure out what they're up to."

"How?"

"I dunno yet."

"Well *that's* brilliant."

"You have a better idea?"

I shook my head. "Where's the thing now?"

"In my suitcase. But I'm gonna keep it with me, in case they show up here while we're gone."

Matt ducked back into the room and went over to his suitcase. I was staring out at the street, looking for the weird guys.

"What are you two talking about?"

Suzana's voice, which I was not expecting, made me bang my head on the window frame for the second time that day.

"You have to stop doing that," I said. She was leaning out her window, looking amazing. Even though I had a lot of stuff on my mind at the moment, it occurred to me, somewhere deep inside my brain, that Matt was right: I had zero chance with her. Zero.

"Who are those guys?" she said. "And what is it they want?"

"What guys?" I said.

She rolled her eyes. "The guys you were just talking about with Matt. Who want the thing Matt is getting from his suitcase."

"Oh," I said. Because that's how good I am at thinking up things to say under pressure.

"Is it the weird guys from the plane?" she said.

"Yeah," I said, because I couldn't think of a reason not to.

"What's the thing?"

"We don't—"

"It's a detonator," said Matt, sticking his head through the window and holding out the box for Suzana to see. "We think."

"We don't know," I said.

Suzana was staring at the box.

"But they want it back bad," said Matt. "They were chasing us near the White House."

"*What?*" said Suzana.

So we told her about the guys chasing us around the White House, and how we got away, and how somebody called the bus company and found out what hotel we were in. When we were talking it sounded crazy even to me, but Suzana listened like she totally believed us.

When we were done, she said, "So they're coming here." She seemed kind of excited about this.

"Yeah," I said. "Apparently."

"So what's the plan?" She said this like she was part of the plan.

"Mainly for now, don't let them get this thing," said Matt.

Suzana nodded. "Okay," she said. "Give it to me." She held out her hand.

"What?" said Matt and I pretty much together.

"They're chasing you guys," said Suzana. "They're not chasing me." Her hand was still out.

Matt and I looked at each other.

"Okay," said Matt, handing over the box.

I said, "Are you sure . . ."

"I'm sure," she said, and she disappeared with the box into her room.

Matt and I looked at each other again.

"Was that a good idea?" he said.

"*Now* you ask," I said.

I looked at my phone. It was time to meet in the lobby for the evening activities. I took one last look out at the street in front of the hotel. It was getting dark. I didn't see the weird guys.

But they were out there somewhere.

I don't remember very much about the evening activities. We ate at a restaurant near the Capitol that specialized in feeding tour groups, as opposed to regular humans who would eat there on purpose. Our three entrée choices were The Executive, which was chicken that could have been fish; The Legislative, which was fish that could have been chicken; and The Judicial, which was meat loaf that could have been seat cushions. Then we went to a concert by a military band that played "pop music," which apparently means music that is no longer popular. The concert was outdoors, and everybody was sweating because the weather was still pretty hot, especially for nighttime.

To be honest I didn't pay much attention to the evening activities because I was busy getting more and more nervous. I kept looking around for the weird guys. I never saw them, but that didn't make me feel any better. By the time we got back on the bus to go back to the hotel, I felt like I was going to throw up. I sat down and leaned over in my seat, holding my stomach, telling myself *Don't puke in front of everybody Don't puke in front of everybody Don't puke in front of everybody . . .*

"Are you okay?"

I looked up and saw that it was Suzana, sitting next to me, in Matt's seat. *Suzana Delgado was sitting on the bus next to me.* This was a violation of all the known physical laws of the Culver Middle universe: A hot girl like Suzana sitting next to a nobody like me instead of with the other hot girls and popular boys. I'm sure this set off a chain reaction of staring, nudging, and texting throughout the bus. I couldn't see, because now I was busy telling myself *Don't puke on Suzana Don't puke on Suzana Don't puke on Suzana . . .*

"Wyatt?" she was saying. "Are you all right?"

"I'm fine," I said.

"You look like you're gonna puke," said Matt, sliding in behind us and leaning forward.

"I'm not gonna puke," I said. "But I *am* worried about what's waiting for us back at the hotel."

"That's what I wanted to talk to you about," said Suzana. "I think we need a plan."

"What kind of plan?" I said.

"For if those two guys show up at the hotel. Looking for this." She pointed to her purse.

"Why would they want your purse?" said Matt, who, as I have pointed out, can be an idiot.

Suzana rolled her eyes. "Not my *purse*. The thing. It's in there."

"Ohhhh," said the idiot.

"So here's what we do," said Suzana. "If they show up at the hotel, you pound on the wall to my room three times." She sounded pretty excited about the idea of them showing up at our hotel.

"Then what?" I said.

"What do you mean?"

"I mean, what happens after we pound on your wall?"

She frowned. "I don't know yet. It depends on the situation."

I blinked. "That's our plan?"

"So far, yes."

I nodded thoughtfully, because I couldn't think of anything to say.

"I like it," said the idiot.

"Good," she said. "Remember, three pounds on the

wall." She got up and walked back to the hot and/or popular section of the bus.

"She's really nice," said Matt, moving up and sliding in next to me. The bus was moving now.

"I guess," I said. But I was starting to think the main reason Suzana wanted us to pound the wall was to make sure she didn't miss anything exciting. Such as us getting killed.

"Listen," I said. "If those guys show up, I'm gonna tell Mr. Barto."

"I thought we decided—"

"I changed my mind. This is getting too weird. I'm gonna tell him. I don't care if we get sent home."

Matt was quiet for a few seconds. "Okay," he said.

The bus got back to the hotel and pulled into the driveway. We both looked out the window before we got out, but we didn't see the weird guys, or anybody else: The street was quiet. Matt and I stopped just inside in the hotel doorway and took a careful look around the lobby. But the only people there were in a sad little line to check in—a tired-looking couple with a crying baby waiting behind a couple of businessmen, who were waiting behind a tall man in a hat and overcoat and a short dumpy blond lady in a red dress and purple shoes talking to the guy at the front desk. Other than that, the lobby was empty.

Mr. Barto and Miss Rector gathered us all together and

gave us a lecture about how we were to stay in our rooms and they would be patrolling the hallways and anybody caught breaking curfew would be in Serious Trouble. Then we headed for the elevators. The Hot/Popular clot drifted past. Suzana worked her way over and whispered, "Seen anything?"

"No."

"Okay," she said. She held up three fingers. "Remember the signal."

"Okay."

Her clot drifted away. Matt and I and some other losers got on an elevator. As soon as the door closed Cameron Frank released a pretty spectacular fart, even by his standards, but I was too tense to laugh.

I felt a little safer once we got to our room. We got into our pajamas and figured out where to sleep. There were two beds, plus a sleeper sofa, plus a cot, which was where I ended up. We turned on the TV and sat around doing stuff on our phones, with Matt or me getting up every couple of minutes to look out the window and not see anything.

A little after ten thirty somebody pounded on the door, which made Matt and me both jump up, but it was just Mr. Barto telling us to turn off the TV and the lights and go to bed. He was still wearing his backpack; I think maybe he slept with that thing on.

We turned the lights off and the TV sound down and went back to our phones. I looked out the window a couple more times, but I was getting pretty tired, and I was beginning to feel like we were going to be okay, at least for the night. I closed my eyes and my mind started drifting around, the way it does when you're falling asleep. I drifted back to Miami, and getting on the plane, then kind of went through the whole insane day, ending with getting back to the hotel and being scared that the weird guys would be waiting for us. . . .

Suddenly I sat up. I was wide awake now.

I looked around the room. The TV was still on, with the sound down. Victor and Cameron were asleep in the two beds. Matt was asleep on the sofa bed. I got off the cot and walked quietly over to Matt. I poked him and whispered, "Wake up."

His eyes opened. "What?"

"They're here."

"What?"

"*Shh.* Whisper."

"Where are they?" he whispered.

"In the lobby. We walked right past them, but their backs were turned so I didn't see their faces. I don't think they saw us."

"You *saw* them? Why didn't you say anything?"

"I just now figured out it was them."

"You're sure?"

"Yeah. Remember when we came in tonight? The man and the lady at the front desk?"

He frowned. "Yeah, but that was a man and a lady."

"Did you happen to notice what the man was wearing?"

He thought about it for a second. "A coat?"

"Right. A long coat."

"So?"

"So it's warm out. Way too warm for that coat. That's like a heavy winter coat. He's wearing it to cover himself, especially his tattoos. He had a hat on, too. He doesn't want us to recognize him."

"But he was with a lady."

"He was with somebody in a dress."

"With blond hair."

"Or a blond wig."

"But why do you think that was—"

"The *shoes*. Do you remember the shoes on the 'lady'?"

"No."

"They were purple. I didn't really think about it at the time. But they were definitely purple."

"So?"

"Purple shoes with a red dress?"

"Those don't go together?"

I rolled my eyes. "No. And guess what the little weird guy was wearing on the plane."

"What?"

"Purple Crocs."

"You're sure?"

"Positive. I thought it was weird, a grown-up wearing Crocs."

We heard a rustling in one of the beds. Cameron was sitting up.

"What's going on?" he said.

"Nothing," I said.

"Okay," he said. He got up and shuffled into the bathroom.

Matt leaned toward me and whispered, "Okay, say that was them, in the lobby."

"It *is* them. They're here."

"Okay, but they don't know what room we're in."

"I think maybe they do. I think that's why they were talking to the old guy at the front desk. They were finding out what room we're in. Maybe even bribing the old guy to give them a key."

"But they don't know our names."

"Yes they do."

"How?"

"Remember the air marshal? On the plane? He asked us both what our names were. The weird guys were right there."

"Oh man, that's right."

"Yeah."

"So what do we do now?"

I didn't have an answer for that. I was thinking.

And while I was thinking, somebody knocked on our door.

CHAPTER 6

For a few seconds Matt and I just stared at each other's frozen faces in the flickering TV light.

Finally Matt said, "Ohmigod, what do we do?"

I put my finger in front of my mouth. *Shh.*

I looked at the room phone. Should I call somebody? Who?

More knocks on the door. Harder this time.

I realized something: *If they had to knock, that meant they didn't have a room key.*

"What do we do?" Matt said again.

"Nothing," I said. "We stay quiet. They can't get in."

Then the toilet flushed. *Cameron. I forgot about Cameron.*

He came out of the bathroom. I waved my arms to get his attention, but he wasn't looking my way.

A voice outside the door said, "Hotel security! Open up!"

Cameron turned toward the door.

"No!" I said, jumping up.

Too late. Cameron was turning the doorknob.

The door banged open and Cameron staggered backward as the big guy, wearing the hat and overcoat, shoved him into the room. Right behind him was the little guy, wearing the red dress and the blond wig, looking like the world's ugliest lady. He closed the door behind him and turned on the room lights as the big guy kept shoving Cameron backward.

"Hey!" said Cameron.

"Shut up," said the big guy, pushing Cameron down onto his bed. Victor, in the other bed, was waking up. He blinked, looked at the two weird guys, started to say something, then decided not to.

The little guy walked past the big guy and stood in front of me and Matt. He looked really ridiculous in the wig, but this did not seem like a good time to say so.

"Where is it?" he said.

"Where is what?" said Matt. Have I mentioned that he's an idiot?

The little guy sighed. He pointed to the big guy and said,

in a reasonable-sounding voice, "Would you like him to beat your head on wall?"

"Not really," said Matt.

"Good. So tell me, where is it?"

Matt looked at me, which caused the two weird guys to look at me, which was unpleasant.

"We don't have it," I said.

The big guy stepped toward me. This was even more unpleasant. I took a step backward. My back was now pressed against the wall.

"What do you mean, you don't have it?" said the little guy.

"We gave it to somebody."

"Who?" said the big guy.

I didn't answer.

The big guy raised his fist. It was a big fist. It looked like a catcher's mitt. I raised my hands in front of my face.

"Who did you gave it to?" the big guy said. "TELL ME NOW." He emphasized those last three words by pounding the wall right next to my head, BANG, BANG, BANG.

"Next time," he said, "I don't hit wall."

I was thinking as hard as I could for a person who was very close to peeing his pj's. On the one hand, I didn't want to sic these two lunatics on Suzana. On the other hand, I didn't want the big guy to turn my brain into guacamole.

"One more time," said the big guy, raising his fist again. "Who'd you give it to?"

"I . . . I . . . I . . ."

"You *what?*"

I honestly didn't know what I was going to say after "I," and I never will know, because that was when the window opened. We all looked that way and saw Suzana, in her pajamas, standing on the hotel driveway roof and leaning through the window. She was holding up her iPhone.

"I called 911," she said. "The police are on the way."

The big guy and the little guy looked at each other.

Suzana said, "You guys are in major trouble."

The big guy gave a *What now?* look to the little guy. The little guy grabbed Matt's arm and said "*You.* You took it, and you will tell me where it is *right now.*"

"It's not in this room," said Matt.

"WHERE IS IT?"

Right then we heard a siren, *bwoop bwoop,* nearby. Everybody looked toward the window.

"Told you," said Suzana.

The big guy went over to the little guy and said, "We must go."

The little guy looked really unhappy.

Bwoop bwoop. The siren was closer.

"Okay," said the little guy. "We are going. But we

are taking you." He yanked Matt toward the door.

"Hey!" said Matt.

"Let him go!" yelled Suzana. She was climbing through the window. Matt was still struggling and yelling. The big guy walked over and reached his hand back, like he was about to hit him. Matt stopped struggling.

"No more noise," the big guy said. "Or you get hurt." He grabbed Matt's shoulders and shoved him toward the door.

Bwoop bwoop.

Suzana was in the room now.

"YOU LET HIM GO!" she shouted. It occurred to me that she wasn't just taller than me; she was also way, *way* braver.

The little guy turned around and looked at her, then me, Cameron, and Victor. "We will let him go when you give it back." He looked down and saw an iPhone on the sofa bed. He picked it up. "Is this yours?" he said to Matt.

Matt nodded. He was crying, trying not to make noise, tears dripping off the end of his nose.

The little guy turned back to the rest of us.

"If you tell the police anything about us, anything, you will never see your friend again, you understand?" He looked around at us. *"You understand?"*

We all nodded. Cameron also farted, but I think it was just nervousness.

The little guy held up Matt's phone, looked right at me, and said, "We will message you. You will do what we say."

Then they were pushing Matt out the door. I caught a glimpse of his teary red face looking back at me, scared to death.

And then they were gone.

CHAPTER 7

Somehow, Suzana got rid of the police. She went back to her room before they got to the hotel, and I don't know what she said to her roommates, but they backed up her story, which was that they called 911 because they saw a guy on the driveway roof outside their window. A cop went out on the roof and looked around, but he didn't find anything. The cops came to our room and asked us if we'd been out on the roof, and we said no, and the girls in Suzana's room said it wasn't us, it was definitely a man, but they didn't get a real good look at him.

In the end the police told us to keep the windows locked,

and we said absolutely we would. Mr. Barto and Miss Rector stuck around a while looking unhappy, but they couldn't really yell at us about anything, so finally they left. In all the excitement and confusion they didn't notice that Matt was missing, and of course we didn't point that out to them. As soon as they were gone Victor and Cameron started asking me a million questions about who the weird guys were, and what they were looking for, and generally what the heck was going on. I told them about the weird guys, and how they had acted on the plane, and how Matt took the thing from the little guy's backpack, and how the weird guys were after us to get it back. When I was finishing up we heard tapping on the window. I opened it and Suzana climbed into our room. She was wearing a Miami Heat parachute sack.

"Have you heard from them?" she said.

"No," I said.

"We need a plan," she said.

"Maybe we should tell the police," I said.

"You mean, like, the police who were just here, and we finally got rid of them?"

"I know, but maybe that was a mistake. Those guys have Matt."

"And they said if we told the police, they'd kill him."

"They didn't say they'd kill him."

She rolled her eyes. "They said we'd never see him again,

Wyatt. What do you think they meant? That they're taking him to Disney World?"

I was getting a really bad feeling in my stomach. "So what do you think we should do?"

"I don't know yet," said Suzana. "I'm thinking."

Victor, who'd been quiet, said, "Where is it?"

"Where's what?" I said.

"The thing they want."

Suzana took off the parachute sack. "In here."

"Can I see it?" he said.

She pulled out the box and handed it to Victor. He looked at it, turning it around in his hands.

I said, "Matt thought it was a detonator."

"I don't think so," he said.

"So what is it?"

"I'm not sure. But I think this"—he pointed to the little Plexiglas dome—"is a laser."

"Cool," said Cameron.

I said, "Why would those guys have a laser?"

"I dunno," said Victor. "But I think this might be a military thing."

"Those aren't military guys," said Suzana.

Victor took a picture of the box with his phone. "My dad's an intelligence analyst with the Southern Command," he said. "He might know what this is."

"Okay," said Suzana, "but don't tell him where you got it, until we get Matt back."

"Which we have no idea how we're gonna do," I said.

Suzana was about to say something, but before she could, my phone made the sound of Homer Simpson belching, which is the sound I use for texts.

"Did your phone just burp?" said Suzana.

I looked at the screen, and my stomach flipped over. "It's a text from Matt."

"What's he say?" said Suzana. She, Cameron, and Victor crowded next to me to see the screen. It said:

police?

"What does that mean?" said Cameron.

"I guess they want to know if the police are around," I said.

"Answer no," said Suzana.

I typed **no** and sent it. Then we waited. It felt like a long time, but it was probably only a minute or two. Then my phone burped again.

tomorow 10am boy scout statue bring it

"What are they talking about?" I said. "*What* Boy Scout statue?"

Suzana and Victor were both thumbing their phones.

"There's a Boy Scout Memorial," said Victor.

"On something called the Ellipse," said Suzana.

"That is a weird statue," said Cameron, looking at Suzana's phone.

"Tell them we'll meet them," said Suzana. "Text okay."

"But how're we gonna meet them?" I said. "Don't we have some museum thing tomorrow?"

"Smithsonian Natural History Museum," said Victor, still thumbing his phone. "It's about a mile from the Boy Scout statue."

"But how will we get away?"

"We'll figure that out," said Suzana. "Tell them okay."

I texted **ok**. We waited again. Finally the phone burped.

com alon or you do not see frend agan NO POLIC

"They're not very good at spelling," said Cameron, taking over for Matt in the role of idiot.

"How do we know Matt's okay?" I said.

"Ask them," Suzana said.

I thumbed my phone:

is matt ok? can we talk to him?

We all stared at my screen, waiting. We stood there looking at it for five minutes, hardly breathing.

The phone did not burp.

Finally Suzana said, "We need a plan."

CHAPTER 8

We finally got to bed around two a.m., but I don't think anybody got much sleep. I definitely didn't. I kept thinking about Matt. When he was around, he was unbelievably annoying, but now that he wasn't around, I was really wishing that he was.

I also wished that I'd been braver when the weird guys were in our room. At least Suzana tried to stand up to them. I didn't do anything. I just stood there and watched them shove him out the door.

I kept seeing his face, looking back at me.

The other thing I was thinking about was our plan for

getting him back. It was really mostly Suzana's plan. Her idea was that we should get Matt back—that was the most important thing—but also try to get video of the weird guys, so we could give it to the police. We all agreed that we would definitely tell the police everything after we got Matt back, even if it meant getting in trouble and getting sent home. Whatever those guys were planning to do, we knew it couldn't be good.

I guess I did finally fall asleep, because suddenly I woke up and it was light outside and Cameron was yelling at me to wake up or I was going to miss breakfast. He and Victor were already heading out the door. I got dressed and ran downstairs to the dining room and got on the end of the line for the buffet, which featured scrambled eggs from like 1950.

I wasn't hungry anyway. I sat at a table with Victor and Cameron and pretended to eat, but mainly I snuck peeks over at Suzana in the Hot/Popular area. She was wearing the Miami Heat parachute sack. I caught her eye once, and she winked at me. Then she went back to being hot and popular. She looked totally amazing, not tired or stressed at all, like ho-hum, just another normal day on the class trip instead of a day when we had to try to get our friend back from two weird kidnapper guys who for all we know were trying to blow up the White House.

Our first problem was getting through the head count.

They counted us whenever we got on the bus to make sure we were all there. If they noticed that Matt was gone, they'd want to know where he was, and we'd have a big problem, because if we told them what happened, they'd call the police, which was exactly what we wanted to avoid.

The good news was, the head count was usually done by Mr. Barto, who is not the world's most organized person, which is why we thought our plan (which was really Suzana's plan) might work. What we did was, when we got on the bus, Cameron and I sat together in the fifth seat on the left side, and Suzana sat in the fifth seat on the right, across from us. Victor sat alone a few rows back. So Mr. Barto came down the aisle counting heads. He counted me and Cameron, then turned and counted Suzana. Which was when she went into action.

"Mr. Barto," she said, making her eyes all big and help-less, "can you help me? I can't get the window open."

"Sure," he said, all manly. She got up and he got into the seat and opened the window, which of course Suzana could have done. While Mr. Barto's back was turned Cameron slipped out of our seat and went back to sit with Victor. Mr. Barto stood back up and Suzana thanked him and flashed him a big Suzana smile. He said you're welcome, then went back to counting heads, which meant that he counted Cameron's head twice.

84

So far, so good.

Our bus parked in a long line of buses near the Smithsonian National Museum of Natural History, which is a giant stone building near a bunch of other giant stone buildings, which seems to be the main kind of buildings they have in Washington. It was a longish walk to the front entrance, and the weather was already hot, so we were pretty sweaty by the time we got inside. It was a little after nine a.m., which meant we had less than an hour to escape from the class trip and get to the Boy Scout statue.

The museum was pretty cool, I guess. It was huge inside, and there were life-size models of big animals, like an elephant and a whale, and some dinosaur skeletons. But I was too nervous to pay attention to the exhibits. I was keeping an eye on Suzana, who was slowly drifting back farther and farther from the front of the group, pretending to be fascinated by museum stuff we were passing. I drifted back with her, followed by Victor and Cameron, until we formed a little group in the back, falling farther and farther behind until we were the tail end of the class.

I looked at my phone: It was nine twenty-one. We had thirty-nine minutes to get to the statue. Up ahead, the front of the group was going around a corner into a hallway.

"Get ready," said Suzana.

We slowed down, then stopped just before the corner.

When the group was out of sight, we turned around and started walking fast toward the exit. In two minutes we were walking out the entrance back into the heat.

"Which way?" said Cameron.

Victor had his phone out, looking at a map. "This way," he said, pointing right. We all started running. I glanced at my phone: it said *9:24.* We weren't going to have much time.

Of course Suzana was the fastest runner. She plays club soccer, and she's really good, like she is at everything. Victor, Cameron, and I had a hard time keeping up with her. Also the temperature was like sixteen thousand degrees. We ran past some more giant stone buildings and turned a couple of corners, and then Victor said, "We're almost there. It's across the street and up that way, where those trees are." He pointed to the right.

I looked at my phone.

"It's nine forty-two," I said. "We have eighteen minutes."

"Okay," said Suzana. She looked at me and said, "You're sure you don't want me to do it?"

I shook my head. "We talked about this last night. They said the message was for me. If they see you, they might freak out."

She nodded, but she wasn't happy. She actually *wanted* to be the one to go meet the weird guys. I definitely did not, but I didn't see how I could get out of it.

Suzana took off the parachute bag and handed it to me. She looked at Victor and Cameron and held up her phone. "You guys ready?"

They both said yeah and held up their phones.

"We all take video," she said. "But we *stay out of sight*. And if anything bad happens, we all call 911."

They nodded. I tried not to throw up.

"Okay, Wyatt," she said. "You go over first. Stand by the statue. We'll go down the street and come to the statue from the other direction, so when they see you they won't see us. But we'll be watching you. Good luck."

I just nodded, because my mouth was too dry to talk. I went to the corner and waited for the light to change. I kind of hoped it never would. But it did.

I took a deep breath, let it out, and started across the street.

CHAPTER 9

I crossed the street and turned right, toward where Victor had pointed. I really didn't like being alone. I felt like I had a nest of snakes squirming around in my stomach.

It took me a couple of minutes to reach the Boy Scout statue, which was on a big stone pedestal next to a round water pool that didn't have any water in it. The statue was pretty weird. It was a Boy Scout wearing a uniform and hiking along with a walking stick in his hand. On either side of him, a little behind, are a man and a woman. What makes it weird is, the man isn't wearing any clothes, except for a tiny piece of cloth that barely covers him. He's like, "Here we are, hiking along on a Boy Scout hike, and by the way I'm naked."

Sometimes I do not get art.

There were a bunch of tourists in the area kind of milling around; also some homeless people. But I didn't see the weird guys, and I didn't see Matt. I stopped in front of the statue and turned around slowly, trying to look casual. I didn't see anybody I recognized. I was holding my phone in case the weird guys texted me.

I stood there for maybe a minute, which felt like an hour.

My phone burped.

I looked at it.

other side

I figured that meant I was supposed to go around to the

back of the statue. I looked around. I still didn't see the weird guys, but obviously they could see me, which was creepy. I started walking around the statue. I hoped Suzana and the other guys were keeping me in sight. My legs felt like spaghetti.

There were a few people on the other side of the statue—some people sitting on the grass eating, a lady with a stroller, some kids on skateboards—but what I noticed right away was the person on a bench maybe twenty yards behind the statue, facing away from it. I couldn't see the person's face, but I could see that, in the hot sunlight, the person was wearing a black overcoat, just like the one the big weird guy had on the night before. And if that wasn't enough of a giveaway, the person was wearing a blond wig, exactly like the one the little weird guy had worn. There might as well have been a sign pointing at the bench saying SUSPICIOUS PERSON.

At first I figured it had to be one of the weird guys, but then I had another idea: *Maybe it was Matt.* Maybe they told him to sit there until they got their box back. I stood there, staring at the person, trying to decide what to do. My phone burped again.

put it by trsh

I looked around. There was a trash basket off to my right. I went over and set the parachute sack on the ground next to it. Then I stood still and waited. I had sweat dripping into my eyes. A skateboarder went past me. The stroller lady was coming my way.

My phone burped again.

walk 2 seat DO NOT TRN AROND

I figured that meant walk toward the bench. I started walking toward the bench. When I got about ten feet from it my phone burped.

STOP

I stopped and stood there staring at the back of the blond wig. All around me I could hear people talking, yelling, laughing; they had no idea what was happening. Sweat was pouring down my face, stinging my eyes, but I didn't dare move. I stood there waiting, but I didn't know what I was waiting for.

"Matt," I whispered, to the back of the wig.

Nothing.

I tried again, louder.

"Matt, is that you?"

Nothing.

I looked down at my phone. Nothing.

I wondered where Suzana was. I really really wanted *somebody* to tell me *something*.

My phone burped. I looked down, and when I saw the message I suddenly felt cold.

u did not com alon

Oh no.

In front of me, the blond-wigged person was standing up. The person reached up and took off the wig, then took off the coat, then turned around.

It wasn't Matt.

It wasn't one of the weird guys, either.

It was a homeless guy, his hair all straggly, with a gray beard and raggedy clothes.

I said, "Who're you?"

He said, "Who're *you?*"

"Wyatt!" I turned around and saw Suzana running toward me, full speed. Behind her, a ways back, were Victor and Cameron.

Suzana reached me, breathing hard. "Who's he?" she said, pointing at the homeless guy.

"Why's everybody want to know who I am?" he said.

"Where'd you get that wig?" said Suzana.

"Why's that your business?"

"Because I'll pay you five dollars to tell me." She said this without hesitating for a second, like it was a line from a movie she knew by heart.

The homeless guy said, "Okay, gimme the five."

Suzana said, "Tell me first."

He thought about that for a second, then said, "Okay. It

was a big guy. Bald. He told me to put on the coat and wig and sit on this bench, don't move, don't turn around for a half hour. Paid me twenty. Where's my five?"

"Did he have anybody with him?"

"A boy. About his size." He pointed at me.

"Did the boy say anything?"

"No."

"Did he look scared?"

"How do I know? That's enough questions." He held out his hand.

Suzana reached into her pocket and pulled out a five, which she handed to the homeless guy, who took it and walked away.

Suzana looked at me and said, "So where are they?"

"I dunno," I said. "But they knew I wasn't alone." I held up my phone so she could see the last text.

"Hey," said Victor. "The sack. It's gone."

We looked back toward the trash can near the statue. The parachute sack wasn't where I'd set it down. I ran over and looked on the other side of the can. It wasn't there, either. I looked around. There were plenty of people around, but nobody had the sack that I could see.

"Who took it?" I said. "Did anybody see?"

They all looked at each other.

"Weren't you guys taking video?" I said.

"Yeah," said Cameron. "But I figured the guy on the bench was one of the weird guys, and the idea was to get video of them, right? So when you walked to the bench I was aiming at you. I kind of forgot about the sack."

"Me too," said Suzana. Victor nodded.

"Oh, man," I said.

"Wait a minute," said Victor. "From where I was standing, I think I might have the trash can on the video."

"Let's look," I said.

We squeezed around Victor and made some shade so we could see his phone screen. He started the video, and we saw me set the sack down next to the trash can. Then we saw me walking toward the bench and stopping behind it. Victor was right: We could still see part of the trash can at the very left-hand edge of the screen. We saw a couple of skate-boarders go past, then the lady with the stroller. When the lady got to the trash can, she stopped for a second and bent over. We couldn't see what she did. But it wasn't hard to figure out.

"The lady took it?" said Cameron.

"Back up," Suzana said to Victor. "And zoom in on her face."

He did, but we couldn't see much, because the face was almost totally covered by a bunch of brown hair.

"I think that's a wig," said Suzana.

I was getting a bad feeling.

"Back up some more," I said. "Okay, stop there. Now zoom in on her feet."

"Her feet?" said Victor.

"Yeah."

"Okay," said Victor, zooming.

And there they were.

The purple Crocs.

"It's him," I said. "The little weird guy."

"So," said Victor. "Now they have Matt *and* the box."

Nobody said anything for a few seconds. Then Cameron said, "They're smarter than we are."

"Shut up," said Suzana.

I said, "Now we have to call the police."

Nobody argued. I raised my phone to call 911. I tapped 9, then 1, and then . . .

And then my phone burped.

We all crowded in to read the text.

if u cal polic u nevr se frend agan

"They really can't spell," said Cameron.

"Shut up," said everybody else.

"Ask them how we can trust them," said Suzana.

I typed:

y shud we beleive u?

We waited.

u hav no chos

"Chos?" said Cameron.

"Choice," said Suzana.

"They have a point," said Victor.

I was about to ask what I should text back, but before I could my phone burped again.

we giv frend bak 2 days IF NO POLIC

"I don't trust them," said Suzana. "Tell them we want proof Matt's okay."

I texted:

we want proof our friend is ok

We all stared at the screen. I don't think I was breathing. Thirty seconds went by, then, *burp*:

look @ stret

"Stret?" said Cameron.

"Street, maybe?" I said.

A horn honked three times.

We looked over at the street.

"There," said Victor. "On the other side."

A silver minivan was stopped at the curb. The front driver's side window was down. The little guy was at the wheel, holding a phone, watching us. He'd taken the wig off. When he saw us look his way, he said something. The rear window slid down.

And there was Matt. He looked terrified.

I could see the big guy right next to him in the backseat.

I waved at Matt. He didn't wave back. The window went back up, hiding his face.

The minivan started moving. In a few seconds it was gone.

"What do we do now?" I said. *"What do we do?"*

"Right now," said Victor, "we have to get back to the class trip."

Suzana looked at her phone. "Oh, man," she said. "We gotta hurry."

We started running. I felt weird, like my brain was spinning around. I wasn't looking where I was going. I kept thinking about Matt's face. I stumbled over something and almost fell. Suzana caught my arm and held me up.

"Thanks," I said.

"Don't worry," she said. "Matt'll be okay."

"We don't know that," I said.

"We'll figure this out," she said. "We'll think of something. But right now, we have to get back, so focus on that, okay?"

"Okay," I said. But all I could think about was what Cameron said.

They're smarter than we are.

CHAPTER 10

e made it back to the Smithsonian just in time and slipped in with the rest of the group in the gift shop. From there we went outside to a park and the teachers gave us box lunches containing sandwiches made from some meat that nobody could definitely identify, although one kid who moved to Miami from West Virginia swore, and I don't think he was kidding, that it was squirrel. I gave mine to Cameron. Even if it had been real food, I couldn't have eaten it. My stomach was a mess.

We sat on the grass a little ways from everybody else—me, Cameron, Victor, and Suzana. At this point just about everybody had noticed that Suzana was hanging with us losers instead of the Hot/Populars, but she didn't seem to care.

"Okay," she said. "We need a plan."

I said, "I'm still thinking maybe we should call the police."

"Really?" she said. "You saw what they texted. If we go to the police, we don't see Matt again. You think they were kidding?"

"I don't know," I said.

"You want to take that chance? That they'll kill him?"

When she said "kill" it felt like somebody kicked me in the stomach.

"No," I said. "But what are we supposed to do? Nothing? Not even tell his parents?"

"If we tell his parents, they'll tell the police. Telling his parents could be killing him."

Another kick to my stomach.

"So we do *nothing*?"

Cameron added, "They said they'd let him go in two days."

"Why should we believe them?" I said. "They said they'd let him go at the statue."

"Yeah," said Victor. "But you told them you'd be alone."

Another kick. I was going to need a new stomach.

"So," I said, "we just sit around for two days, hoping they're not lying?"

"Maybe we can find them," said Suzana. "We saw their car."

"A silver minivan," said Cameron. "Probably only about ten million of those in Washington."

"You have a better idea?" said Suzana.

"He has an iPhone, right?" said Victor.

We all looked at him.

"Find My iPhone!" said Suzana. She looked at me. "Does he have that?"

"I dunno," I said. "But even if he does, what if it's not turned on? Or the weird guys turned it off?"

"We have to hope they didn't," said Suzana.

I said, "Don't we need a password or something?"

"We do," said Victor.

"You don't know the password?" said Suzana.

"No," I said.

"Could you figure it out?"

"I could try."

"All right," said Suzana. "When we get back to the hotel, we work on that."

I was starting to realize that Suzana was the kind of person who really liked having a plan.

We finished eating—or, in my case, watching Cameron eat my squirrel sandwich—and then we walked to our next thing, which was, surprise, a giant stone building. I wouldn't be surprised if the rotation of the Earth got messed up from all this stone being dug up somewhere else and moved to Washington.

This particular giant stone building was the National Archives, which is where they have the Declaration of Independence, the Constitution, and a bunch of other historic important things. I'm sure it's great as far as archives go, but I don't really remember anything about it, because the whole time I was thinking about Matt. I kept wondering whether he was okay, and what I should be doing, and what I'd want people to be doing for me if the weird guys took me instead of him.

We finally got out of the Archives and walked back to the bus. Mr. Barto did another head count, but Suzana tricked him using *exactly* the same trick she did the first time, making her eyes big and pretending she couldn't work her window.

Girls have this *power*. To be honest, it's a little scary.

Once the bus was going Victor motioned for me, Cameron, and Suzana to talk with him, so we all leaned in.

"Okay," he said. "My dad called me when we were in the National Archives. I sent him a picture of that thing, and he—"

"What thing?" said Cameron, still filling in for Matt in the role of idiot.

"The electronic box those guys were after," said Victor.

"Ohhh," said Cameron.

"What'd your father say?" said Suzana.

"First of all, he wanted to know where I saw it. He *really* wanted to know where I saw it."

"What'd you say?" I said.

"I lied. I said it was a picture I saw on the Internet, and I wondered if he knew what it was. And he did, right away."

"So what is it?" I said.

"It's a jammer. It uses a laser to jam laser-guided missiles so they miss their targets. My dad says it's super high-tech and restricted, and only the U.S. military is supposed to have it. They use it over in Afghanistan and around there."

"Those guys aren't U.S. military," I said.

"No," said Suzana.

"Why would they want to jam missiles?" said Cameron.

My stomach turned over.

"I know why," I said.

They all looked at me.

"Matt was right," I said. "They're targeting the White House. That's why they were looking at aerial photos on the plane. And that's why they were hanging around the White House."

"But that doesn't make sense," said Suzana. "The box doesn't *shoot* missiles. It *jams* missiles. How can it attack the White House?"

"It can't," said Victor, seeing it now. "But it can jam missiles coming *from* the White House."

"Why would missiles be coming from the White House?" said Cameron.

"To defend it," said Victor.

"From what?" said Cameron.

"From another missile," said Victor. "Or a plane. Or whatever those guys are planning to attack it with."

"Ohhh," said Cameron.

"This is bad," I said. "This is really, really bad. We have to tell somebody now."

"What about Matt?" said Suzana.

I pictured his face, when he was in the weird guys' van. Scared to death. I shook my head, trying to make the picture go away. "We have to do *something*."

"Okay," said Suzana. "Here's what we do."

We looked at her. I could tell that she—or at least part of her—was absolutely loving this. It almost made me mad, except I was glad that *somebody* had a plan.

"We have two days," she said. "So we use them to try to find Matt and rescue him. If we can't, we have to tell the police. But we do everything we can to find Matt first." She looked around at the three of us. "Everybody okay with that?"

We nodded. We had a plan:

Rescue Matt in two days.

Or . . .

I didn't want to think about it.

CHAPTER 11

We didn't have much time when we got back to the hotel, because we had to get ready to walk to dinner, which was at an allegedly Italian restaurant near the hotel. We had pizza. Usually, this is a good thing. Most kids like pizza because it's always pretty much the same and not weird, so you're usually safe ordering it. But this "Italian" restaurant made the worst pizza in the history of the universe. I'm pretty sure that the tomato sauce was actually ketchup, and I am almost positive that the cheese—I bet if you tried this in Italy they would put you in jail—was Kraft Singles. The worst part was the pizza dough, which I think they got from Home Depot. It was a weird combination of rubbery and hard. It was like biting into a Frisbee. I gave mine to Cameron. I wasn't really hungry anyway.

After dinner it was dark and we went on our evening activity, which was a Historic Ghost Walk, led by Gene. He took us through a bunch of neighborhoods, and every now and then he'd stop in front of some random old building and tell us about some spooky thing that supposedly happened there a long time ago. He did his best to sound scary, but I couldn't really get into it. First of all, I had a lot of stuff on my mind. Second, people my age grow up playing video games where we fight these really gory battles against realistic monsters that squirt green blood when you decapitate them, and we watch movies where people's eyeballs explode or they get eaten by giant alien insects or they're captured by a lunatic with a basement dungeon laboratory where he surgically turns them into human lobsters or whatever. So we're not going to get too scared about some house where the ghost of President Zachary Taylor's daughter allegedly sometimes closes a door.

The Historic Ghost Walk lasted a long time, so we didn't get back to the hotel until almost ten p.m. Maybe a minute after we walked into our room Suzana tapped on the window and climbed in, carrying her iPad. She was already on the Find My iPhone site.

"What's Matt's Apple ID?" she asked.

"Same as his e-mail," I said. "MightyMatty."

She looked at me. "Seriously?"

"Yup."

She rolled her eyes and tapped it in.

"Now," she said. "Any luck with his password?"

"Not really," I said. I'd been thinking about it, but I hadn't come up with anything.

Cameron said, "I read that the most common password people pick is the word 'password.'"

"Yeah," I said, "but you'd have to be a complete idiot to ..." Then I remembered this was Matt we were talking about. "Try it," I said to Suzana.

She tapped in *password.*

"Nope," she said.

Cameron said, "Another one is the first five keys on the keyboard: *qwerty.*"

Suzana tried that. "Nope."

We also tried *123456* and *654321* and *123123.* All nopes.

Suzana looked at me. "Does he have a pet?"

"No."

"Maybe some singer or movie or video game he really likes?"

Before I could answer Victor said, "Do we know where those guys are from?"

"Why?" I said.

"I'm just thinking, while you guys are trying to figure out the password, maybe I could see what I could find out about them."

"Well, they're foreign," said Cameron.

"Wow," said Suzana. "That's a brilliant observation."

"Really?" said Cameron.

"No," said Suzana.

But Cameron had reminded me of something. "On the plane," I said, "the air marshal asked the little weird guy where he was from, and he told him."

"Where was it?" said Victor.

I tried to remember. "It was something stan," I said.

"Afghanistan? Pakistan?"

"No, not them. It was one I never heard of."

Suzana went to Google maps. "Okay," she said, "Here's the stans . . . Kazakhstan . . ."

"No."

"Kyrgyzstan . . ."

"No."

One by one she went through the stans, but none of them sounded familiar.

"That's all of them," she said. "No, wait." She zoomed in. "Here's a little tiny one: Gadakistan?"

"That's it!" I said. "Gadakistan."

"I'll look it up," said Victor, tapping his phone.

Suzana was back on the password problem. "So?" she said. "Matt's favorite singer?"

"He's not really into music," I said.

"How about video games?"

"He likes Halo," I said. "He sucks at it. He gets killed in like twenty seconds. But he plays it a lot."

Suzana tried *Halo* and *halo*. "Nope."

"Okay," said Victor, looking at his phone. "According to Wikipedia, Gadakistan is this brand-new country. They just had a war of independence, and the head military guy, Gorban Brevalov, declared himself the leader. Nobody knew much about him, but he declared that he was an ally of the United States, which apparently was a big deal."

"So they're friendly to us?" said Suzana. "So why would they—"

"Hang on," said Victor. "*Brevalov* is friendly to us. But there's this rebel group that's still fighting him, called Ranaba Umoka. It means *Dragon Head*."

"Okay," said Suzana, "but I still don't see why . . ."

"Wait a minute," I said. "Dragon Head?"

"Yeah," said Victor. "Their symbol is a picture of a dragon's head."

"That's what the little weird guy had in their backpack!" I said. "On the plane. A dragon head. Remember?"

"That's right!" said Suzana. "So you think the weird guys are part of this Dragon Head group?"

"Why else would they be carrying a dragon head around?" I said.

"Okay," said Victor. "So what we have is guys who belong to a group fighting against an ally of the United States, and they have a missile-jamming device they're not supposed to have, and they're here in Washington poking around the White House."

We all looked at each other, letting it sink in.

"They're planning something bad," said Cameron.

"Wow," said Suzana. "Again, a brilliant observation." She looked at her watch. "We do not have a lot of time to find Matt. We *really* need to figure out that password." She looked at me. "Think hard, Wyatt. What else is Matt into?"

I thought hard, then snapped my fingers. "*SpongeBob SquarePants.*"

"Seriously? He still watches that?"

"Every single day. Try SpongeBob and SpongeBob SquarePants."

She tapped her iPad. "Nope ... and nope. What else?"

I tried to think, but nothing came. For a while nobody said anything. I was starting to realize how tired I was, how tired we all were. We just sat there, staring at nothing. A bad feeling was filling the room, a failure feeling.

Then Cameron said, "Did you use a capital B?"

"What?" said Suzana.

"When you typed 'SpongeBob.' It's one word, but the 'Bob' part has a capital B."

"And you know this because?"

Cameron blushed. "I'm a huge *SpongeBob* fan myself."

"Why am I not surprised," said Suzana. She tapped on the screen. We waited, watching her.

"That's it!" she said.

Victor, Cameron, and I jumped up and went over to look at the iPad. The screen showed a compass with an arrow moving back and forth, over the word *Locating* . . .

"Let's hope he has it turned on," said Suzana.

Suddenly the compass disappeared, and there was a map.

Then a green dot appeared in the middle of the map.

"There's Matt," said Suzana.

CHAPTER 12

e stared at the dot for a couple of seconds.

Then Cameron said, "Where is that?"

Suzana zoomed the map out a little.

"It's near the Capitol," she said. She switched to satellite view and pointed. "There's the Capitol dome, see?" She zoomed in. The green dot was on the roof of a smallish house to the east of the Capitol in a neighborhood made up of a whole lot of smallish houses all squeezed together in blocks.

"How far away is that?" I said.

She moved the map and pointed. "Our hotel is here." She

zoomed partway back out. Now we could see our hotel and the green dot.

"That's not that far," I said.

"Maybe a mile," said Victor.

We stared at the map a little more, nobody talking. Then Suzana looked at me and said, "Ready?"

"For what?" I said.

"To go get Matt."

"You mean now?"

"Yes, now, while we know where he is. You ready?"

The truth was, I didn't feel ready at all. I felt like crawling into bed and pulling the covers over my head and closing my eyes until this whole mess went away. But there are some things you just can't do, and one of them is tell Suzana Delgado, who you are discovering is basically a Navy SEAL disguised as a hot eighth-grade girl, that you're afraid to go with her to rescue your friend.

"Yeah, I'm ready," I said.

"Okay," she said. She looked at Victor. "You stay here."

"Why?" said Victor.

"In case Wyatt and I get into trouble," she said. "You can help us get out of it. If we're all there together and something goes wrong, we have no outside help."

My stomach did not like the way that sounded.

Victor nodded. Cameron said, "So I'll go with you guys?"

Suzana looked at him, and I could tell what she *wanted* to say, which was something like, *We'd really rather you didn't go, because you're kind of an idiot and a lot of the time you smell like a badly maintained public restroom.* But—give her credit—she didn't say that to Cameron. What she said was, "I guess."

"What's your plan for getting Matt out?" said Victor.

"Depends what the situation is," said Suzana. "We'll figure that out when we get there." She seemed really confident about that.

We made sure everybody had everybody else's phone number. Suzana snuck back to her room and told her roommates she was sneaking out and they should cover for her, which of course they would because she was Suzana. Then she came back to our room. We turned out the room lights and I opened the door and peeked into the hall.

"Nobody out there," I said.

"Let's go," said Suzana.

The three of us stepped into the hall; Victor closed the door behind us. I started toward the elevator.

"No," whispered Suzana. She pointed the other way. "Stairs."

We trotted down to the end of the empty hallway, past a bunch of rooms full of sleeping kids who were having a normal class trip and not sneaking out of the hotel in the middle of the night to try to save their friend from Gadakistani terrorists planning to attack the White House.

We went down the stairs, which let us out in the back part of the lobby. It was empty; there wasn't even anybody behind the front desk. We walked fast across the lobby and went out of the hotel and down the driveway to the sidewalk. The weather was definitely cooler than it had been, and the wind was picking up. Suzana was in front, walking fast, so Cameron and I almost had to run to keep up with her. She turned right, walked to the end of the block, and stopped. She took out her phone and went to Find My iPhone.

"That way," she said, pointing.

"We're gonna walk?" said Cameron.

"Yeah," said Suzana. "It's only one-point-two miles, and if we take a taxi they might see it pulling up."

"Why don't we take a taxi part of the way?" said Cameron.

"Look," she said, "if you don't want to do this, you can go back to the hotel."

"No, I just . . ."

He didn't finish, because Suzana had turned around and was already walking. I followed her, and Cameron followed me. There was no question who was in charge of this operation.

We moved fast, Cameron and I half-trotting to keep up

with Suzana. There was hardly any traffic, and hardly any-body on the sidewalks; the stores and businesses were almost all closed. After about ten minutes we could see the Capitol dome. Suzana veered down a street to the right. We made a few more turns, Suzana watching her phone screen, and soon we were in a neighborhood of the smallish row houses we'd seen on the map. The streets were darker now, and there was nobody on the sidewalks.

Suzana stopped and pointed to her phone. "It's in the next block."

"So what now?" I said.

"First of all, we stay totally quiet. *Totally*."

At exactly that moment, Cameron farted.

"Sorry!" he said.

"If you do that again," she said, "I will kill you."

It didn't sound like she was kidding.

"I'm not kidding," she said, removing all doubt.

"Okay," said Cameron.

"We're going to walk past the house," said Suzana. "We don't stop. We check it out and keep walking. We'll stop at the other end of the street and figure out a plan. Okay?"

Cameron and I nodded.

"Okay, let's go."

She started walking, checking her phone every few sec-onds. After maybe fifty feet she slowed a little and pointed to her right. I looked, and my stomach jumped: parked at the curb, facing us, was a silver minivan.

Suzana kept going. In the middle of the block she slowed down again and pointed at the house directly to her left. It was a redbrick house, narrow and two stories high, like all the others on the block. It was attached to the house on the left, but there was a small alley between it and the house to the right. There were no lights on anywhere that I could see. The house had a front porch with a couple of metal chairs on it, looking over a small front yard with a FOR RENT sign stuck in the grass.

Suzana kept walking to the end of the block, where she turned and waited for me and Cameron.

"What do you think?" she said, looking at me.

The truth was, I wasn't thinking anything, because I was expecting Suzana to have a plan.

"Well," I said, trying to think of something, "we need to figure out where Matt is."

"Right," she said.

"I bet it's the basement," said Cameron.

"Why?" said Suzana.

"Because that's *always* where they keep prisoners."

"You mean in movies."

"Right."

"This isn't a movie."

"That's true," said Cameron.

"But it kind of makes sense," I said. "That he'd be in the basement. They could lock him down there, and there's no windows for him to climb out of."

"True," said Suzana, a little unhappily because it meant she was agreeing with Cameron.

"Okay," I said. "Say he's locked in the basement. How do we get him out?"

"There's an alley on the side of the house," said Suzana. "We sneak back there and check the windows. There might be one unlocked. Or we could maybe break one."

"But they'd hear us," said Cameron.

"So we'll create a diversion."

That was *definitely* a line from some movie, but I didn't point that out. What I said was, "What kind of diversion?"

"Like we pound on the front door, make some noise out there. While they're checking to see what it is, we sneak in and let Matt out of the basement."

She made it sound totally simple.

I said, "So who's going to create the diversion?"

"I will," said Cameron. I did not expect that. He sounded really brave. As soon as he said it, I wished I'd said it.

"Okay," said Suzana. "You hang out front. We'll go around the back and check it out. When we're ready I'll text you, and you start making noise. Try to get them to come out of the house if you can. The longer you can keep them busy, the more time we have to find Matt."

"Okay," said Cameron.

"Let's go," said Suzana.

We walked back to the house. It was still dark. The street was still empty and quiet.

For a few seconds we just stood on the sidewalk, looking at the house. You know how, in like every horror movie, there's a scene where the people who are about to get hacked apart by a chain saw maniac or turned into human lobsters in the secret basement laboratory come to a creepy house, and everybody watching the movie is thinking DON'T GO INTO THAT HOUSE YOU IDIOTS but they always do anyway? That's what it felt like to me—a don't-go-into-that-house moment.

But I could not say that to Suzana.

Besides, Matt was in there somewhere.

Matt was in there somewhere.

"Everybody ready?" whispered Suzana.

Cameron and I nodded.

"Okay," whispered Suzana.

We started walking toward the alley.

CHAPTER 13

The alley smelled even worse than the hotel room. Also it was really, really dark. It was so dark I couldn't see Suzana, who was right in front of me, which I found out when I bumped into her.

"Sorry," I whispered.

"*Shh.*"

We inched forward trying not to inhale the swampish smell. When we got to the end there was a little bit of light from the house on the next street over. We could see that the backyard had a high wooden fence around it, with a gate to the alley. The gate had a latch, but there was no lock. Suzana quietly lifted the latch and pushed the gate. It creaked, and she froze, but nothing happened, so she slowly pushed the gate open and we went into the backyard.

"Oh my God," whispered Suzana, breaking her own silence rule. Not that I blamed her.

Because the backyard wasn't empty.

In fact, it was totally, fully occupied.

By a dragon.

The body had to be twenty feet long, with big spikes along the back and a long tail coiled behind. It had clawed feet and big wings on either side. And the head . . . well, I'd seen the head before, on the plane.

"What in the world?" whispered Suzana.

"No idea," I said.

We touched it. The skin was some kind of nylon-y material, held up by some kind of frame underneath. You could tell that even though it looked huge, it was pretty lightweight.

"This is just *weird*," whispered Suzana.

"Yeah."

We pondered the weirdness for a few more seconds, then Suzana said, "Okay, let's see how we get inside."

There was a wooden porch on the back of the house, with steps going up to it. We went up the steps really carefully, to keep them from creaking. There was a back door, with windows on either side. I tried the door; locked. Suzana went to the window on the left and pressed her face against it. She motioned to me, and I looked in. There was just enough light coming through the window that I could see it was the kitchen. We tried lifting the window; it was locked. We went to the window on the other side and looked in; it was an empty room. We tried lifting the window.

It was unlocked.

Slowly, we slid it up. We got it open about three inches when it got stuck. We gave it a little shove; nothing. I was about to give it a harder shove, but Suzana stopped me. She put her mouth right next to my ear and whispered "Diversion."

I nodded. She was right. Opening the window was about to get noisy.

"When we get in, look for the basement," she whispered.

I nodded again.

She took out her phone a tapped a text to Cameron:

now

Then we waited. We stood by the window with our shoulders just barely touching, which should have been the highlight of my life—*My shoulder is touching Suzana Delgado's shoulder*—but I really can't say I was enjoying the moment. Sweat was trickling into my eyes and I don't think I was breathing at all.

Nothing was happening. It felt like at least a minute had

passed since Suzana sent the text, and there was no noise from the front. I decided Cameron must have chickened out. I didn't really blame him. It was insane to be deliberately trying to wake up a pair of crazy guys who . . .

BANG

Even at the back of the house, it sounded loud—the sound of a metal porch chair slamming into the front door. This was followed by Cameron's fists pounding on the front door, and Cameron yelling something I couldn't make out.

So much for him chickening out.

"Now," whispered Suzana, and we both shoved up on the window as hard as we could. It opened with a bang, but that got covered up by all the noise coming from the front of the house. Suzana went through the window and I was right behind. Now we were in the empty room. There was a door to our left, which opened onto a hallway. We stuck our heads out and looked right. At the end of the hallway was a door next to some stairs.

"I bet that's the basement door," said Suzana.

We heard men yelling upstairs and feet pounding. We pulled back and watched. A couple of seconds later the little weird guy came down the stairs, with the big guy right behind. At the bottom of the staircase they turned right, away from us, into what I guess was the living room, headed for the front door. The diversion was working.

"Come on," said Suzana.

We ran to the door next to the stairs. Suzana tried it; locked. It had those round locks above the knob, the kind you need a key to open.

Suzana stepped back and kicked the door hard. Then I did. Nothing. At the front of the house the banging on the door suddenly stopped. We heard the front door opening and the men going out, shouting. I heard Cameron shouting too, from outside, still diversioning.

"Kick it together," I said. "Near the knob. One, two . . . *three*."

And that time it opened.

And there was Matt.

He was standing near the top of the basement stairs, looking terrified and then suddenly very happy.

"Wyatt!" he said.

We heard the weird guys shouting again. But now they were closer. They must have heard us and quit chasing Cameron. *They were coming back into the house.*

"Come on!" said Suzana. I grabbed Matt and yanked him up the stairs. We followed Suzana, running to the door at the back of the house. It was also locked, but it was the kind of lock you could open without a key, just by turning a knob. Suzana fumbled with it. The men's shouting got louder behind us. Suzana got the door open and we ran out onto the porch. There was shouting and pounding feet in the hallway. We turned right and ran past the dragon. We got through the gate just as the weird guys reached the back porch. We went into the alley, which was still completely black. Suzana was in front; I had Matt by the arm and was dragging him behind me. We reached the end of the alley. I looked back; it was too dark to see the weird guys, but I could hear them coming. We ran to the street, turned right, and started running down the middle of the street as fast as we could. We looked back and saw that the weird guys had reached the end of the alley and were looking around for us. They spotted us, looking back at them, but they didn't start running. They could see we were too far away; we'd already proven that we could outrun them.

We were going to get away. *We were going to get away.*

And then I saw Cameron.

Oh no.

He was standing in the open front door of the weird guys' house, looking in, pounding on the door frame.

He hadn't seen us come out of the alley. He thought the weird guys—and we—were still inside the house.

He was still creating a diversion.

I yelled, "Cameron! Cameron! Run!"

He didn't hear me. Didn't even turn around.

Didn't suspect a thing until the big guy grabbed him from behind and carried him into the house.

The little guy was still in the street, looking toward Suzana, Matt, and me.

He stared at us for maybe five seconds.

Then he went into the house and closed the door.

CHAPTER 14

e stood in the middle of the street, looking at the door.

"What do we do now?" I said.

"I don't know," said Suzana. Which was not like her.

Lights were coming on in some of the other houses on the block.

Suzana turned to Matt. "What will they do to him? Did they do anything to you?"

"No," said Matt. "They locked me in the basement and fed me frozen pizzas. I mean, they microwaved them, but they started out frozen. You know how they say frozen is the same as delivery, but it's not, but it was okay, as long as I picked off the mushrooms, because those are—"

"Shut up about the pizzas," said Suzana.

"Okay," said Matt.

"Did they hurt you?" said Suzana.

"No," said Matt. "All I did was eat pizza and watch TV and sleep. They told me they'd let me go when they were done."

"Done with what?"

"They didn't tell me."

The front door of a nearby house opened. A guy stepped out onto the porch and stared at us.

"We need to get out of here," said Suzana.

We ran to the end of the block, away from the weird guys' house, Suzana in front, Matt and me trying to keep up. When we rounded the corner Suzana slowed down to a fast walk.

"How'd you guys find me?" puffed Matt.

"Your phone," I said.

"Ohhh, right. Well, thanks. For coming to get me, I mean."

"You're welcome."

"So now we're gonna call the police, right?"

Suzana stopped, turned, looked at me.

"I think we'd better," I said.

"I don't know," she said. "What if they . . ." She shook her head.

"What if they what?" said Matt.

"They said they'd kill you if we called the police."

"*Kill* me?" said Matt.

"They didn't say kill," I said.

"That's what they meant," said Suzana.

"Wait," said Matt. "You were talking to them?"

"Not talking," I said. "Texting from your phone."

And right on cue my phone rang. I dug it out of my pocket and the three of us looked at the screen. It wasn't a text: It was a FaceTime video call from Matt's phone.

"Answer it," said Suzana.

I slid my finger across the answer bar, and a few seconds later there was Cameron's face on the screen. Somebody else was aiming the phone at him. There was a bright light shining on his face. He looked really scared.

"Wyatt?" he said.

"Yeah, it's me. I'm with Suzana and Matt." I moved under a streetlight so he could see our faces better. "Are you okay?"

"They're really mad," he said. His voice was shaky. "They said you better not tell the police. They said if you tell the police . . ."

He stopped, about to cry. We could hear somebody saying something to him, but we couldn't make out what it was.

Cameron nodded, swallowed, and said, "Wyatt, *please*, don't tell the police. Promise, okay? They're listening."

"Okay," I said. "I promise we won't tell the police."

And then Cameron's face was gone.

I said, "Cameron? Hello?"

But the call was over.

I looked at Suzana. "Now what?"

"I don't know," she said, for the second time. "For now I guess we should go back to the hotel, before they figure out we're missing."

"We're just gonna leave Cameron?" said Matt.

"We're going to figure out how to get him out," said Suzana. "But we're not going to do something stupid now and get him hurt."

"I still think we should call the police," said Matt.

"You just heard me promise I wouldn't," I said. "We made the same deal when they had you, and we got you out, didn't we?"

"Yeah," said Matt. But he didn't sound convinced.

The truth was, I wasn't convinced either. But I'd made a promise.

"Okay, then," said Suzana. "Back to the hotel."

CHAPTER 15

e made it back to the hotel and snuck up to the room without any trouble. Victor was still awake, looking worried. We told him what happened with Matt and Cameron at the weird guys' house, which made him look more worried.

"So now they have Cameron," he said.

"Yeah," I said.

"This is bad," he said.

"What do you mean?"

"My dad called me," he said. "Really late. He had a lot more questions about the picture of the jammer I sent him.

He wanted to know where exactly on the Internet I saw it. I made up a story about how I didn't actually see it on the Internet myself, but somebody sent it to me and I didn't know where they got it but I would try to find out."

"Why's he so interested?" said Suzana.

"The picture I sent him. He showed it to some people where he works, military intelligence people. They blew it up and enhanced it and they could read the serial number. There aren't many of those things. And they knew exactly which one this one was. It was stolen off a helicopter in Afghanistan, and they've been trying to track it down because they really, *really* don't want this technology to get out. So according to their informants it was sold to a guy who sold it to another guy who sold it to another guy in Miami. And that's where they lost the trail."

"So that's why the weird guys were in Miami," I said. "They were getting the box."

"Yeah," said Victor. "And speaking of them, I've been doing some more research about Gadakistan, and—"

"About whatistan?" said Matt.

"Gadakistan," said Suzana. "That's where those guys are from."

"So anyway," said Victor, "remember I told you the leader of Gadakistan is a guy named Gorban Brevalov?"

Suzana and I nodded.

"Well, guess who's going to be visiting the White House?"

"Seriously?" said Suzana.

"Yes."

"When?"

"Tomorrow. Actually, now it's today. This afternoon."

"So that's why they're here," I said.

"Looks like it," said Victor.

"Waitwaitwait," said Matt. "What are we talking about?"

"Okay," I said. "You missed some stuff. The box you stole from the little guy's backpack is a jammer. It jams laser-guided missiles, so they miss their targets. We think these two guys plan to use it to jam the missiles that protect the White House, so they can attack it."

"Attack it with what?"

"We don't know that," said Suzana. "But now we know when. The leader of Gadakistan is going to be at the White House this afternoon. It looks like our guys are planning to attack it then."

"But they're from Gadakistan too," said Matt. "Why would they attack when their leader is there?"

"Because they're against him," said Victor. "They belong to a rebel group Ranaba Umoka. It means *Dragon Head*, which must be why they were carrying one. They—"

"Wait a minute," I said.

Victor looked at me.

"Suzana and I saw it tonight," I said. "The dragon head."

"Where?"

"At the house where they were keeping Matt. In the backyard. Attached to a dragon."

"*What?*" said Victor.

"Yeah," said Suzana. "There's this giant weird dragon made of nylon or something."

"Why would they have a dragon?" I said.

"Maybe they're going to use it in one of those Chinese parades," Matt said. "You know, where a bunch of people march inside a giant dragon puppet."

"Oh yeah, I've seen those," I said. "Hey, maybe that's how they're planning to attack the White House!"

"Yeah, right," said Suzana. "Because the Secret Service would *totally* let a giant dragon puppet with people under it march right up to the White House."

It did sound pretty stupid when she put it that way.

Victor was staring at us.

"Is it heavy?" he said.

"Is what heavy?" I said.

"The dragon. Did you try to lift it?"

"Actually, I did, a little," I said. "It's not heavy at all. In fact it's really light."

"Why does that matter?" said Suzana.

Instead of answering, Victor tapped his computer for a

few seconds. Then he said, "Okay, this is from the Wikipedia article on Gadakistan: 'Among the most popular traditional activities are kite-building and kite-flying. Many villages pride themselves on creating large, elaborate kites which are entered in regional and national competitions.'" He looked up at us. "I bet the dragon is a kite."

"It's pretty big," said Suzana.

"Kites can be big," said Victor.

"Wait a minute," said Matt. "You think they're going to attack the *White House* with a *kite*?"

"I think it's possible," said Victor.

"But this is the *White House*," said Matt. "You don't think they'll notice a couple of weird guys lurking around there with a giant dragon kite?"

"Maybe not," said Victor, "if there's a whole bunch of *other* big kites around."

We all looked at him. I snapped my fingers.

"When we went by the Washington Monument," I said. "Those guys were flying those big kites."

"Right," said Victor. "Gene said there was going to be a big kite festival on the Ellipse. It's right next to the White House."

Suzana said, "Okay, but how much damage can they do with a kite? Even a big one?"

"A lot," said Victor. "If it's carrying a bomb."

"It could carry a bomb?"

"I bet it could," I said. "One of the kites we saw near the Washington Monument lifted a guy off the ground."

"So that's their plan," said Suzana. "They're going to use their dragon kite to bomb the White House."

"I think it makes sense," said Victor.

"So we tell somebody this, right?" said Matt. "Like the Secret Service?"

"Wrong," said Suzana. "First of all, I don't think the Secret Service would take us seriously. I bet people are always calling them and making crazy threats. They're not going to believe some kids with a story about a kite. And secondly, we can't risk having those guys hurt Cameron."

"So what do we do?" I said.

"We stop them," she said. "We know what they plan to do, and we know when they plan to do it."

"Maybe," said Victor. "But even if we're right, how do we stop them?"

I knew exactly what Suzana was going to say, and I was exactly right.

"We'll figure that out when we get there," she said. "The main thing now is, we should try to get some sleep. It's really late, and we're going to be busy tomorrow."

Which turned out to be the understatement of the year.

CHAPTER 16

I fell asleep in like two seconds, but I had a bunch of dreams, all bad. In the last one I was being chased by a giant flying dragon, which caught me in its mouth and started shaking me. Fortunately, before it could kill me, it turned into Victor. Unfortunately, Victor wasn't in the dream; he was the real Victor, shaking me and telling me to get up.

"Really?" I said. I could have slept for a week.

"We're supposed to be at breakfast by eight," he said, heading for the door with Matt.

I looked at my phone and groaned: 7:55. I got dressed as fast as I could and ran down to the dining room, where

Victor, Matt, and Suzana had saved a seat for me at a table for four. We were all too tired to care about the fact that the entire eighth grade was now openly speculating on how it could be possible that Suzana Delgado, goddess, seemed to be voluntarily spending all her time with the Dork Patrol.

"Nice of you to join us," said Suzana.

"Do we have a plan yet?" I said.

Suzana looked at Victor.

"As far as I can tell from the news stories on the Internet," he said, "Brevalov will be meeting the president at three o'clock, and after that they're going to have a press conference outside in the Rose Garden."

"So they'll be outside sometime after three," said Matt. "Which is when those guys will use the kite bomb."

I said, "And our plan is . . ."

"We go to the Ellipse at, say, two thirty," said Suzana. "We find the kite guys, and we stop them."

"How?"

"However we have to. Cut the kite string, tackle them . . ."

"*Tackle* them?"

"Whatever it takes. At that point we could probably even tell the police, since they'd both probably be there, which means they couldn't do anything to Cameron. And they'll have the bomb."

"Suzana, I don't know. That one guy's pretty huge."

"But there's four of us."

"Yeah, but . . ."

"But what? Are you scared?"

I looked down. "I guess I am," I said.

"I am, too," said Matt. "If it makes you feel any better."

It didn't, but I appreciated the gesture.

"Well, if you're afraid," said Suzana, "you don't have to go."

"No," I said, "I'm going." At that moment I realized I had managed to do the worst possible thing, which was commit myself to maybe getting killed by the Gadakistan maniacs and *still* look like a coward to Suzana.

Suzana looked at Victor. "What's the class trip schedule today?"

Victor looked at his phone, where he had the schedule. "After breakfast we go to the National Zoo."

"Why're we going to a zoo?" said Matt. "We already have a zoo in Miami."

"The one here has pandas," said Victor.

"So?"

"So for some reason everybody makes this huge deal about pandas. I don't know why. They never actually do anything except eat and poop. But they're really famous."

"Yeah," said Suzana. "They're like the Kardashians of zoo animals."

"So after the zoo, then what?" I said.

Victor looked at his phone again. "We eat lunch at noon at the zoo. Box lunches."

"Again?" said Suzana.

"I'd rather eat panda poop," I said.

"Hey," said Suzana, "judging from the other box lunches, that might be what we get."

"Then at one," said Victor, ignoring us, "we take the bus to our next thing, which is . . . a tour of the U.S. Capitol. Which is kind of like the zoo, when you think about it."

"Okay," said Suzana. "We'll ride the bus from the zoo to the Capitol. Then we'll escape from the class trip, go to the Ellipse, and stop the kite guys."

"Won't they eventually notice we're not on the Capitol tour?" said Matt.

"Yeah," said Suzana. "But by the time they notice, it'll be over, and we'll be able to explain that we had to do whatever we end up doing."

Whatever *that* meant.

We finished breakfast and got on the bus. This time Suzana didn't even have to ask Mr. Barto to open her window; he just did it. She totally had him trained.

I almost fell asleep on the bus ride to the zoo. I felt like I hadn't really slept since the class trip started. Which was more or less true.

140

The zoo was okay, I guess. It was definitely better than walking around inside another giant stone building. The day was sunny, but cooler than the past few days, with a steady breeze blowing.

We saw the famous pandas, or at least one of them. It was eating leaves the whole time I watched. At least it didn't poop.

I can't tell you much about the other animals we saw. I was too tired, and too worried about what might happen, to pay attention. I stumbled around the exhibits like a zombie. When it was finally time for lunch we sat at some picnic tables and they handed out the box lunches, which contained something called "veggie wraps." They looked like some kind of poisonous sea creature that attaches itself to an underwater rock with suckers.

After we finished mostly not eating our box lunches, it was time to get back on the bus. We rode to Capitol Hill and parked near a bunch of other buses. Then we walked to the Capitol and got on a long line to go through security. Suzana, Victor, Matt, and I stood together so we could figure out our plan, by which I mean so we could listen to Suzana tell us our plan.

"Okay," she said. "We'll do what we did in the Smithsonian museum."

"I wasn't there," said Matt. "What'd we do?"

"We hung back at the end of the group," said Suzana. "Then when the group went around a corner, we took off."

"And that worked?"

"Yup."

"How do we get to the Ellipse?" said Victor.

"We'll take a taxi," said Suzana. "I have money."

So that was our plan.

The security line inched forward until finally we got into the visitors center, where we watched a movie about how historic the Capitol is. I kept looking at Suzana to see if it was time to escape, but she kept shaking her head, and she was right. The group was too clumped together for us to get away.

After the movie we got an official guide, who led us up some stairs into the Rotunda, which is the inside of the big dome of the Capitol. It's really big, and according to the guide many historical things happened there. I realize I'm sounding pretty stupid here, but that's basically all I can remember. I kept looking at Suzana, and she kept shaking her head. We couldn't move to the end of the line because the whole group was still more of a clump than a line. Plus every time I turned around, Mr. Barto seemed to be there.

From the Rotunda we went into Statuary Hall, which is a big room with a bunch of statues of famous dead historical people. When the guide started giving her talk,

Suzana motioned for me, Victor, and Matt to come over to her.

"This is the last stop on the tour," she whispered. "We have to go now."

"How?" I said.

She looked around. "One at a time. Go back the way we came in. We'll meet in the visitors center and go back out from there."

Matt started to ask a question, but Mr. Barto was giving us the eyeball.

"I'll go first," whispered Suzana. "Then Wyatt, Victor, and Matt." She turned away, pretending to listen to the guide telling us about the statues. She also started drifting to the outside of the clump. A minute later a big tour group came by, and as they passed Suzana detached from our clump and let herself get absorbed into theirs. In another minute she was on the other side of Statuary Hall, on her way back toward the Rotunda.

My turn. I decided to do what Suzana did, and it worked. I slid into a passing group and slid out the other side. I walked quickly to toward the Rotunda, kind of hunched over, expecting any second to hear Mr. Barto yell my name. But nothing happened, and in a couple of minutes I was back downstairs in the visitors center, where Suzana was waiting. Victor was there a minute or two later, and then Matt.

We were off the class trip now. Outlaws.

We left the visitors center and headed for a major-looking street in the distance, figuring we could get a taxi there. We passed a couple of Capitol police officers, but they didn't pay any attention to us outlaws. To them we were just four kids on a class trip. They'd seen a million like us.

The street turned out to be called Independence Avenue. It was pretty busy. None of us—not even Suzana—had ever actually hailed a taxi before. We stood on the sidewalk and kind of waved our arms randomly at every taxi we saw, but none of them stopped. Sometimes this was because the taxi already had a passenger; sometimes I think it was because the driver didn't want to stop for a bunch of obviously clueless kids making random arm movements.

Finally a taxi pulled over and we piled in, all four of us in the back. The driver didn't look thrilled.

"We want to go to the Ellipse, please," said Suzana. "Near the White House."

"You have money?" said the driver.

"Yes," said Suzana.

The driver looked like he was hesitating, then he put the taxi in gear and started moving.

Then we heard shouting.

Then a crazy person jumped in front of the taxi, yelling at the driver to stop. The driver shouted something in a foreign

144

language and jammed on the brakes, or else he would have hit the crazy person.

The crazy person was Mr. Barto.

He must have seen us sneaking away. His face was red and sweaty. He looked like his head was going to explode.

"Oh, no," said Victor.

Mr. Barto ran around the left side of the taxi and yanked open the back door.

"GET OUT OF THAT TAXI!" he yelled. "NOW!!"

He reached in and grabbed the closest person, which happened to be Matt, and yanked him onto the sidewalk.

"OUT!!" he shouted again. "GET OUT!!!"

Victor, Suzana, and I scrambled out of the backseat. The taxi driver was yelling something about money. Mr. Barto yelled something back about calling the police. The driver made a really unfriendly gesture and shouted something in a foreign language, which I doubt was a compliment, then stomped on the gas and roared away.

Mr. Barto turned his red face to us, the four runaways, and said, "JUST WHERE DID YOU THINK YOU WERE GOING?"

We all looked at each other. Nobody, not even Suzana, knew what to say.

"I WANT AN ANSWER RIGHT NOW!!"

We looked at each other some more, and then Matt said,

"Back to the hotel?" Which, give him credit, was not a bad lie to come up with on short notice, especially for an idiot like Matt.

"That's right," said Suzana, picking up on it. "I wasn't feeling well, so I asked these guys to take me back to the hotel."

"Really," said Mr. Barto.

Matt, Victor, and I nodded hard, like bobbleheads in an earthquake. Suzana made the same helpless-girl face that she used on Mr. Barto when she was pretending she couldn't open the bus window.

This time it didn't work.

"All right," he said to Suzana. "You want to go back to the hotel, you'll go back to the hotel. And you'll *stay* in the hotel for the rest of the day. You're grounded." He pointed to Victor. "You're grounded, too."

Then he turned to Matt and me.

"I already warned you two, at the airport," he said. "You had your chance. You're off the trip."

"What do you mean?" I said.

"I mean you're going home. *Now.*"

CHAPTER 17

I stood there with my mouth hanging open like an unusually stupid fish, staring at Mr. Barto, telling myself *Do NOT cry in front of Suzana Delgado.*

If I got sent home my parents would kill me. Especially my mom. She would kill me, then she would rush me to the hospital so the doctors could miraculously bring me back to life, and then she would kill me *again*.

Not to mention the problem of the two weird guys who were holding Cameron prisoner and planning to blow up the White House.

I couldn't get sent home. I just couldn't.

"I can't," I said.

"You can't what?" said Mr. Barto.

"I can't go home," I said.

"You don't have a choice."

I looked at Suzana and said, "We have to tell him."

She nodded.

"Tell me what?" said Mr. Barto.

So we told him everything—about the two weird Gadakistan guys, and how Matt took their laser jammer, and how they came to the hotel and took Matt, and how they got their laser jammer back at the Boy Scout statue, and how we went to their house and got Matt out but they got Cameron, and how we saw the giant dragon kite and figured out what the weird guys planned to do, and when.

While we were talking, the rest of the class trip came out of the Capitol. Miss Rector came over and joined our little group; the rest of them stood a couple of yards away from us and pretended they weren't eavesdropping, although of course they were. Nobody knew exactly what was going on, but it was obvious that we had done something seriously wrong, so everybody was pretty excited; there's no entertainment like the entertainment of watching somebody else get in trouble.

Mr. Barto and Miss Rector listened to our whole story without saying a word. When we were done, Suzana said,

148

"So we need to go to the Ellipse and stop those guys, and we might not have a lot of time. But we can't go to the police, at least not yet, because they said they'd hurt Cameron."

Mr. Barto and Miss Rector looked at each other.

"Miss Rector," said Mr. Barto, "what do you think of their story?"

Miss Rector looked at us, and I could see the disappointment on her face. "I think it's the most ridiculous thing I ever heard."

Mr. Barto nodded. "Me, too."

"No!" said Suzana. "It's all true!"

"Really!" I said. "Those guys—"

"QUIET," said Mr. Barto. "I don't want to hear any more about that from any of you. It's bad enough that by sneaking off you could have ruined this whole trip for everybody else. I won't have you insult my and Miss Rector's intelligence with this unbelievable story about mysterious men and their giant attack kite."

Miss Rector was looking around, frowning. "One thing they said was true," she said. "We *are* missing Cameron Frank."

Mr. Barto looked at us. "Where is he? Did he go back to the hotel?"

"We *told* you," I said. "The two Gadakistan guys have him."

He glared at me. "Covering for your friend is only going to make it worse."

"I'm not covering for him! It's the truth."

He shook his head, then turned to Miss Rector. "Obviously we need to locate Cameron. I'll notify the Capitol police, but I have a feeling he probably went back to the hotel. Until we find him, I'm canceling the rest of the day's activities."

This announcement brought loud groans from the rest of the group. The four of us were no longer a source of entertainment; we were now officially The Kids Who Wrecked It For Everybody. Mr. Barto pointed at Suzana and Victor and said, "When we get to the hotel, you two will go to your rooms and stay there. You two"—he pointed at Matt and me—"will pack your suitcases. I'll be taking you to the airport personally."

"Please, Mr. Barto, *please*," I said. "I know it sounds crazy but it's all true, and unless we—"

"QUIET," said Mr. Barto. "I will not stand here and have my intelligence insulted any more by your ridiculous lies." He turned to the rest of the group. "All right, everybody back to the bus."

Everybody started trudging toward the bus. Suzana, Victor, Matt, and I walked in front, feeling the angry glares from everybody else burning into our backs. It had to be the worst feeling I ever had. The weird thing was, the day had turned really nice—bright sunshine, but not too warm, and with the breeze still blowing strong and steady.

A perfect day for flying a kite.

CHAPTER 18

"••• and in all my twenty-seven years of teaching,"
Mr. Barto was saying, "I have never seen *anything* as blah
blah blah as the idiotic stunt you pulled, and now thanks to
your incredibly irresponsible blah blah blah you have jeopar-
dized the blah blah blah."

We were in a taxi on the way to the airport, me and Matt
slumped in the back seat, Mr. Barto in the front seat ream-
ing us out pretty much nonstop since we left the hotel. I
was tuning him out because (a) he was repeating basically
the same thing—namely that we were idiots—over and over,
and (b) I was busy answering texts from Suzana. She and

Victor were in their hotel rooms with a chaperone guarding the hallway, but Suzana, naturally, didn't plan to stay there, which led to this conversation between her and me:

SUZANA: v&i will sneak out windows

ME: then what?

SUZANA: taxi to wh. u meet us there

ME: can't barto with us.

SUZANA: get away

ME: how?

SUZANA: think of something

ME: helpful

SUZANA: have 2 go. cu at wh. b there! dont get on plane!!!

I texted her a couple more times after that but she didn't answer. Probably she was busy sneaking out of the hotel.

I showed the texts to Matt. He whispered, "How're we supposed to get away?"

"I don't know," I whispered.

Mr. Barto was still blah-blah-ing away in the front seat. I stared out the window, thinking hard. My first idea was, when the taxi stopped at the airport we could just jump out and run away. But I realized that Mr. Barto would see us, and he'd yell, and there'd be a lot of police around at the airport, and we'd probably get caught. So I decided to go with my second idea, which was hope that Mr. Barto wouldn't go through security with us, because that way, when we got through and were out of his sight, we would wait a few minutes and then sneak back out of the airport.

I whispered this plan to Matt, and he nodded.

We got to the airport and Mr. Barto finally stopped telling us what idiots we were. That was the good news. The bad news was, when he got our boarding passes he also got a special pass for himself, so he could accompany us through security and take us to the plane. He obviously didn't trust us. Which made sense, actually. We definitely were not trustworthy.

So we got into the TSA security line: Matt and me following Mr. Barto and his giant backpack. We were shuffling forward, slow but steady, heading for the plane that would take us to Miami and Death By Mom, heading farther away from Suzana and Victor and poor Cameron and who knows what it was the Gadakistan maniacs were planning to do.

We were running out of time. I kept thinking about Suzana's text: *think of something*. I was thinking as hard as I could, but nothing was coming to me. Ahead of us a TSA guy was saying the same thing over and over—no liquids or gels, take your laptop out of the case and place it in a separate bin, remove your shoes, belts, and jackets.

Matt tapped my shoulder and whispered, "Wyatt."

"What?" I was annoyed, because I was trying to think.

"I just remembered something."

"*What?*"

"The lighter."

"What lighter?"

"The one I got at that souvenir store. It's in my backpack. The security people are gonna think it's a gun."

I turned around and stared at him, remembering the lighter.

"I have to throw it away, right?" he said.

"No," I whispered. "Give it to me."

"Why?"

"Just give it to me. But don't let anybody see."

Matt reached into his backpack, looked around, pulled out the lighter and slipped it to me. I slipped it into my hoodie pocket and turned around to face Mr. Barto's humongous backpack. It had a zipper pocket on the back with a little Homer Simpson doll hanging on the zipper pull. I looked around to make sure nobody was looking my way, then slowly slid Homer sideways. Mr. Barto moved, and for a second I thought he was going to turn around, but he didn't. I put the lighter inside the pocket and slowly slid Homer back.

"Ooohhh," whispered Matt, just figuring it out.

"When you go through the scanner," I said, "follow me, and keep moving. Don't stop, no matter what happens. Okay?"

"Okay."

We kept shuffling forward. Finally we were at the front of the line. A TSA lady checked our passes and we went over to the conveyor belt. Mr. Barto had us go first. We put our backpacks and shoes on it and went through the big X-ray scanner, with Mr. Barto behind us. On the other side we stood next to the conveyor and waited for our stuff. Mine came, then Matt's. We grabbed it.

Then the belt stopped. I was watching the TSA person running the scanning machine. He was staring at it hard, then he looked over toward us. Then he said, "Supervisor!"

"Put your shoes on," I whispered to Matt. I started putting on mine.

The supervisor came over. She looked at the screen, then over at us. She said something to the scanner guy, who started the belt moving again, just enough to let Mr. Barto's backpack come out. The supervisor pointed to it and said to Mr. Barto, "Sir, is this your backpack?"

"Yes," said Mr. Barto.

"Get ready," I whispered to Matt.

"Is there a problem?" said Mr. Barto.

Instead of answering, the supervisor said something to the scanner guy. Three seconds later there were a half dozen TSA people coming our way. One of them, a big guy, stood right in front of Mr. Barto and said, "Sir, I'm going to ask you to step over there."

"Why?" he said. "What is it?"

"Just step over there," said the big guy, taking Mr. Barto by the arm.

"Follow me," I whispered to Matt. I started walking away, and Matt followed. I looked back: Mr. Barto wasn't looking at us. He was focused on the big guy, and he was starting to freak out.

"Can you please explain to me what this is about?" he was saying.

I saw two police officers—not TSA people, but cops, coming into the security area, walking fast. Then a couple more cops behind them. Mr. Barto had a growing crowd around him. As Matt and I lost sight of him, the last I saw was him waving his arms around and asking what the problem was. It would probably be a few minutes more before he noticed we were gone. He wasn't good at details.

Matt and I were in the airport gate area.

"Now what?" said Matt.

I pointed at a sign off to our left that said EXIT BAGGAGE CLAIM GROUND TRANSPORTATION. "That way." A minute later we were back outside the terminal. We followed the TAXI signs and got into a line. While we were waiting, my phone burped. It was a text from Suzana:

where r u?

I texted back:

leaving airport

My phone burped again:

hurry

I texted back:

where r u?

I stared at my phone, waiting. She didn't answer. We got to the front of the taxi line and got into a cab. The driver did not look thrilled to see that he had two kids for passengers, but he didn't say anything.

I said, "We want to go to the Ellipse, please."

"Where on the Ellipse?"

"Um . . . near the White House, I guess."

He turned around and started driving.

"What do we do when we get to the Ellipse?" said Matt.

"Look for Suzana and Victor. And then find the kite guys and try to stop them."

"How're we gonna do that?"

"I have no idea. Suzana said we'll figure that out when we get there. Which is pretty much what she always says about everything."

"Yeah, and look how well everything worked out."

He had a point there.

We rode quietly for a few minutes, staring out the windows.

Then my phone rang, with the tone I use for actual phone

calls, which I hardly ever get. I pulled it out of my pocket, expecting it to be Suzana. But it wasn't Suzana's phone calling me.

It was Matt's phone.

Which meant it was the weird guys.

My finger was shaking when I slid it across the screen to answer the call.

"Hello?" I said.

"Wyatt, it's me, Cameron."

Cameron!

"Are you okay?" I said.

"Don't talk, just listen. I'm almost out of battery. We made a bad mistake. Those guys—"

Then ... nothing. I said, "Cameron? You there? Cameron?"

Nothing.

"Cameron, what about those guys?"

Nothing.

"That was Cameron?" said Matt.

"Yeah," I said. "I think his battery died."

I tried calling back. No answer.

"What'd he say?" said Matt.

"He said we made a mistake."

"What mistake?"

"I don't know. The phone died before he could tell me. He started to say something about 'those guys.'"

"The Gadakistan guys?"

"I think so. But all he got out was 'those guys.'"

"We made a mistake," said Matt.

"Yeah," I said. "A bad mistake."

 or the rest of the taxi ride I stared out the window, wondering what Cameron had been trying to tell me. *A bad mistake.* What could that mean? That we should have gone to the police in the first place? That we shouldn't have gone to the weird guys' house and broken in? That we shouldn't have let them get the laser jammer back?

And how did Cameron manage to call me on Matt's phone? Did the weird guys accidentally leave the phone where he could get it? Did they let him go? Did he escape? If he *had* gotten away somehow, shouldn't I call the police? But what if he *hadn't* gotten away?

A bunch of questions, no answers.

The taxi was back in downtown D.C. I could see the Washington Monument up ahead. The day was still really nice—no clouds, bright sun, blue sky. As we got closer to the Ellipse, I started seeing the kites—all kinds of shapes and colors fluttering and swooping around in the wind. Below them was a huge crowd—there had to be thousands of people. Somewhere in there, I hoped, were Suzana and Victor. Also somewhere in there were the Gadakistan guys and their Death Dragon. Unless we were totally wrong about that. Was *that* the bad mistake Cameron was talking about?

My phone burped up a text from Suzana:

where r u?

I texted back:

almost there. where r u?

The driver pulled over to the curb and stopped the taxi. He looked back and said, "This okay?"

"Yeah," I said.

He pointed to the meter, which said we owed him $18.72. *Uh-oh.*

You're going to think I'm an idiot, and I guess this was pretty idiotic, but I had sort of forgotten about the fact that when a taxi driver drives you somewhere in his taxi, he expects you to pay him. I wasn't sure how much money I had left, but I was pretty sure it was less than $18.72. I got out my wallet and, trying to look calm, counted my money. I had four dollars and some change.

"Matt," I whispered. "Do you have any money?"

"Yeah," he said.

"Give it to me."

He reached into his pocket and pulled out a small wadded-up clump of bills that were stuck together with what looked like melted chocolate. He handed it to me and I started pulling the bills apart. I could feel the cab driver staring at me. I unwrinkled and counted Matt's disgusting bill wads . . . two, three, four . . .

He had five dollars. Which meant we had nine and my change, which was thirty-six cents.

"Do you have any change?" I whispered to Matt.

The driver was staring harder now.

"I think so." Matthew dug into his pockets and handed me, one at a time, a penny, a quarter, another penny, and two green Skittles. Which brought our total to $9.63, which was not enough to pay the fare, let alone a tip.

Now the driver was giving me a look that reminded me of something that happened involving my parents and a taxi driver one time when my family went to New York City. We landed at LaGuardia Airport and we got into this cab with a driver who smelled like he was carrying a dead squirrel somewhere in his pants. Also he drove like a maniac. My family is used to bad driving, because we live in Miami, where according to my dad they'll give a driver's license to anybody including Csonka, who in case you forgot is our dog. But this New York taxi driver was a whole different level of crazy, honking his horn, yelling at people, swerving all over the road, and the whole time yakking on his Bluetooth in what sounded like Martian. So when we finally got to our hotel my dad made a big point of paying *exactly* what was on the meter, no tip. The taxi driver totally freaked out. He jumped out of the cab and got in my dad's face, yelling in both English and Martian, telling my dad he was cheap, and my dad was yelling back, telling the driver he was a maniac, and a crowd started gathering on the sidewalk to watch. My mom started yelling at my dad to stop acting like a macho teenager and just walk away from this maniac, which I think my dad secretly wanted to do, but he didn't want to look like a chicken in front of all these people. So they kept yelling at each other, and the taxi driver got a little too close and kind of chest-bumped my dad, I think by mistake. My dad, who has never been in hand-to-hand combat with anybody and once knocked himself briefly unconscious on a tree while trying to set up a hammock, staggered backward a couple of steps and then staggered forward. I think he was trying to chest-bump the taxi driver back, but he

164

missed completely, stumbled, and fell face-forward onto the sidewalk, cracking a tooth that later turned out to cost twelve hundred dollars to fix. At this point my mom (I believe I have mentioned she is Cuban) marched up to the taxi driver and—remember, this is the person who was telling my dad to stop acting like a macho teenager—smacked him on the side of the head with her purse, which doesn't sound so bad unless you know that my mom always travels with a major purse containing enough food and medical supplies that if our family got marooned on an uninhabited island, we could survive for months, so when she nailed the taxi driver with it he collapsed like a defective lawn chair. So now there were *two* people lying on the sidewalk with a big crowd gathered around, and some police officers showed up and threatened to arrest everybody but finally decided to let everybody go, I think because they didn't want to have to get into a police car with my mom, who can be loud.

The point is, the look on the D.C. taxi driver's face was reminding me a lot of the look on the New York taxi driver's face when he realized my dad wasn't going to give him a tip. Except my situation was worse, because I didn't even have enough money for the *fare*.

"Is there a problem?" said the driver.

"Um," I said. I have a way with words.

My phone burped up another Suzana text:

meet under big butt

What?

"You owe me eighteen seventy-two," the driver said, pointing to the meter.

"Here's the thing," I said. "We don't actually have the total amount."

"How much do you have?"

I held out my hand with the money and Skittles in it. "We have nine sixty-three."

"I might have some more Skittles," said Matt.

Yes, he actually said that. He probably thought it would lighten up the situation. He was wrong.

"You think this is funny?" the driver said. "You think this is a joke?"

"No," I said. "I'm really sor—"

"THIS IS NOT A JOKE. THIS IS STEALING!"

"Look," I said, "if you give me your address, I swear I'll send you the money."

"No!" said the driver. "You are thieves!" He opened his door and got out.

"What's he doing?" said Matt.

"I don't know," I said. Then I saw a police car parked a little ways up the street. The taxi driver was walking toward it.

"Oh no," I said. "He's going to tell the cops."

"What do we do?"

I was already opening the door. "We run," I said.

I got out of the taxi. The driver looked back, saw us, and yelled. I took off running toward the Ellipse with Matt right behind me. I could hear the driver shouting for the police but I didn't turn around. I felt pretty awful; the driver was right, and we were wrong. Maybe some day I could explain to him about the Gadakistan guys and Cameron and the White House and everything. But this was not a good time.

We ran into the kite festival, trying to lose ourselves in the crowd, which was pretty huge. I stopped and looked back and didn't see the taxi driver. Now we had to find Suzana and Victor. I pulled out my phone and read Suzana's text again:

meet under big butt

"Okay," I said to Matt. "Do you see a big butt?"

"That's one's pretty big," he said, pointing to a lady in jeans who did, in fact, have a major butt.

"I don't think that's what she means," I said. "I think she means a kite."

We looked up at the sky, which was full of kites, all sizes and kinds—birds, bats, butterflies, fish, serpents, squids, angels, planes, rockets, random shapes—swooping around in the wind. They went on and on, all the way across the Ellipse. But I didn't see anything that looked like . . .

"A butt!" said Matt, pointing. "Over there!"

I looked, and there it was, hovering at the far end of the Ellipse—a set of naked buttocks the size of a UPS truck.

We ran, dodging through the crowd, until we were under the butt, where a lot of people were taking pictures of it and selfies with it hovering behind them. A few yards away were the guys flying the butt. They looked like college students, which makes sense, from what I have heard about college students.

"Wyatt!"

I turned and saw Suzana running toward me, with Victor behind.

"We found them," she said.

"The Gadakistan guys?"

"Yeah. They're over there." She pointed. I looked and spotted them through the crowd, maybe fifty yards away. The, big guy was pretty easy to pick out.

"Where's the dragon kite?" I said.

"It's still on the ground. Guess what else they have."

"What?"

"A little portable TV. Victor snuck close and got a look. It's tuned to C-SPAN."

"What's C-SPAN?" said Matt.

"It's a TV channel that shows government things," said Suzana.

"Why would anybody want to watch that?" said Matt.

"Well, I can guess why these guys want to," said Suzana. "They're watching to see when the president and the Gadakistan leader, whatshisname . . ."

"Brevalov," said Victor.

"Right, him," said Suzana. "They're gonna watch C-SPAN and see when they come out of the White House for the press conference in the Rose Garden. That's when they'll launch their kite. Except we're going to stop them."

"By telling the police?" I said.

She shook her head. "They won't believe us. Look at what happened when we told Mr. Barto and Miss Rector."

"Yeah, but now they can see the Gadakistan guys, right there. So they'll know we're telling the truth."

"Wyatt, they'll see two guys with a big kite. On a field full of people with big kites."

She had a point.

"So what *are* we going to do?"

"We're going to watch them until they're getting ready to put their kite up. Then we're going to jump them."

"Jump them."

"Yes."

"As in physically jump on them."

"Yes."

"Suzana, the one guy, he's big. He's *really* big."

"Yes, but there are four of us. We jump on them and yell and just generally make it impossible for them to fly their kite. The police will probably come, and they might even arrest us, but at that point it won't matter, because they won't be able to launch their kite in time. The only thing I'm worried about is Cameron. We don't see him here, and we don't know where he is."

"He called me," I said.

"Cameron did? When?"

"A little while ago. He was using Matt's phone."

"Where is he? Did he get out?"

"I don't know. Before he could tell me anything, the battery died."

"But he must be out of that house, right? If he called you?"

"I guess. But here's the thing: He said we made a bad mistake."

"What? What mistake?"

"The battery died before he could tell me."

"Well, do you have any idea?"

"Maybe he meant we shouldn't have let them get the laser jammer back."

"You think?"

"I can't really come up with anything else that would be really *bad*. Like blow-up-the-White-House bad."

Suzana nodded. "That makes sense. We really have to stop those guys."

"Then we really better get going," said Victor. "Because they're about to launch their kite."

CHAPTER 20

We all looked through the crowd. Victor was right: The big guy was holding the end of a rope attached to the dragon and backing away. The little guy was standing next to the dragon, fiddling with it.

"Come on!" said Suzana. As usual, she didn't wait to see if anybody agreed with her. She just took off running. As usual, the rest of us followed her. She was running like a crazy person, waving her arms and yelling. People were getting out of her way. I was sprinting as hard as I could to keep up, zig-zagging through the crowd.

Then I heard a yell and, out of the corner of my right eye, saw something coming at me.

I was tackled and landed facedown, hard enough to have the wind knocked out of me. Someone was sitting on my back, shouting "Thief!"

The taxi driver. The maniac must have been looking for me and Matt. He was not in a good mood.

I rolled sideways and managed to get out from under him and stagger to my feet. He grabbed my arm and was still shouting about me being a thief. I was trying to talk to him, but I couldn't catch my breath. Matt and Victor had stopped and were yelling at him to let me go. There was a lot of yelling going on. A crowd of people had formed around us; I think they were confused about what was happening. I was yanking my arm as hard as I could but the taxi driver, who was a little guy but strong, would *not* let go. I was still gasping for air, trying to explain that I would get him his money if he would just let me go for a minute so I could go help my friend. But he had me in his grip, and I felt totally helpless as well as breathless, knowing that I had messed up yet again, and left Suzana out there taking on the bad guys all alone.

Except she wasn't. I found that out when I heard her yelling "GET OUT OF THE WAY," and then saw her bust through the crowd headed straight for me and the taxi driver.

You have probably never heard of hong fo. It's a martial art, like karate, kung fu, and tae kwon do, except supposedly harder to learn and just generally more martial. Well it turned out that, in addition to everything else, Suzana was a student of hong fo, and although she was fairly new to it, she had learned an attack move, involving both punching and kicking, named The Raptor, after those really mean dinosaurs with like nineteen thousand teeth that ate a bunch of people in *Jurassic Park*. Suzana executed The Raptor on the taxi driver, who never saw what was coming. One second he was gripping my arm and calling me a thief, and the next second he was lying on the ground holding his head.

"Come on," said Suzana. She grabbed me and pulled me through the crowd. People were getting out of her way, and I didn't blame them.

"Who *was* that guy?" she called over her shoulder.

"A taxi driver," I panted, still trying to get my breath. "We owe him eighteen seventy-two. Plus tip."

"You didn't *pay* him?"

"We didn't have enough money. You don't have twenty bucks you could lend me, do you?"

She looked back at me. It was not an admiring look. "*Now?* Are you *serious?*"

"I just thought—"

174

"LATER!" She was already running again, and once again I was following her. We'd lost Victor and Matt, who were stuck back in the mob around the taxi driver. Up ahead, to the right, the big guy—who was wearing some kind of headset with a microphone—had stretched the rope to its entire length. To the left the little guy, who was also wearing a headset, was lifting up the body of the dragon and then lowering it over himself, so only his legs were showing.

"You grab the kite!" Suzana shouted, pointing toward the little guy. "I'll get him." She veered toward the big guy. Just her. Alone. I don't think I ever felt lamer than at that moment, turning left toward a guy who was no bigger than me while Suzana turned right and ran full speed straight toward a guy the size of a building.

But I did turn left.

The big guy started running with the rope, pulling the dragon. While at the same moment the little guy, under the dragon, ran along with him. They were heading into the wind. I could see the dragon starting to lift.

Suzana, who like I said is a very fast runner, caught up with the big guy and launched herself into the air, planning to execute The Raptor. She looked pretty good right up until the moment when she hit the big guy. She bounced of him like a Ping-Pong ball colliding with a cement truck. The big guy kept right on running with the rope. I'm not sure he even noticed that Suzana Raptored him. It was shocking to see. *Suzana actually failed at something.*

Which meant now it was up to me.

Except I'm not as fast as Suzana, and I wasn't sure I was going to get to the little guy before he launched the kite. He picked up speed, and the big dragon lifted higher; I could see most of the little guy's body now. In a few seconds he'd let go of the kite, and I'd be too late to grab it. I veered right a little, trying to get the best angle. Just a few feet to go . . .

Then the little guy shouted something and the dragon suddenly rose, and I knew I wasn't going to get there in time.

Except he didn't let go. He stayed inside the dragon and rose with it, his legs off the ground now, dangling down. In an instant I realized what their plan was: The little guy was going to *ride the kite over the White House fence.* He would operate the laser thing to jam the White House defense missiles, and detonate the bomb, or whatever they planned to do.

Unless I stopped him.

I still don't totally believe what I did next. Later on I saw a video of it, taken on a phone by a guy at the kite festival, and if I do say so myself it was pretty impressive. I sped up, took two long steps, and dove forward like a football

176

player making a tackle, and somehow I managed to get my arms around the little guy's legs. He screamed something in Gadakistani—probably not "Nice to see you again"—and kicked hard with both feet. It hurt, but I hung on. That was the good news. The bad news was, *the dragon kite was still rising*.

It wasn't rising as fast as before, and it was wobbling, but it wasn't coming down. We were swooping across the Ellipse, with me holding on desperately, partly because I wanted to bring down the kite, but also because I didn't want to fall to the ground. The little guy was yelling and kicking, and I felt myself slipping down his legs, until I was barely clinging to his ankles, and I knew I wasn't going to be able to hang on much longer.

Which was when I felt somebody grab *me*. I felt a pair of arms grab my legs, and the weight of another person pulling me down. Somehow I managed to keep my grip on the little guy's legs. But the weight of two bodies hanging on to him was more than he could handle. Suddenly he screamed and fell out of the dragon. I guess I screamed too as the three of us crash-landed, the little guy in front of me, and me on top of the person who tackled me.

Guess who it was?

Here's a hint: The first thing he gasped out, after we stopped tumbling on the grass, was "Thief!"

That's right. Despite being Raptored by Suzana, *he was still after his fare*. Of all the taxis in Washington, I had managed to get into the one being driven by the world's most determined lunatic. He was lying on the ground, looking pretty beat up, but he was *not* giving up.

"Where is my money?" he gasped.

"I'll *get* you your money, okay?" I said, getting up. "Just *wait* a minute."

At this point a bunch of things happened really fast.

First, the dragon came down. The big guy had seen me pull the little guy out of the kite, so he stopped running and brought the kite in for a landing near where the three of us fell. Then he started running toward us.

Also running toward us were Suzana, Matt, and Victor. Behind them a bunch of people were drifting toward us, because this was probably the most exciting thing that ever happened at a kite festival. I know I was excited. I felt like, for the first time in this whole insane class trip, I did something right. Suzana didn't stop the Gadakistan guys. *I* did. I was feeling good. I was thinking maybe everything was going to be okay after all; maybe I was even going to be kind of a hero. The Kid Who Saved The White House. Maybe I would even get a medal!

This was assuming the big guy didn't kill me first. He got to us in a hurry, but ran past me and knelt down next to the

178

little guy, who was lying in the grass, moaning. They talked in Gadakistani, then the big guy stood up and came over to me and shouted, "You have broke his arm! His arm is broke!" His face was all red and sweaty, and he looked like he was going to pick me up, wring my neck, and punt my lifeless body over the Washington Monument, which I think he could probably do.

"Good!" said Suzana, arriving just in time.

The big man turned to her. "Good? *Good?* Why is good?"

"Because now you can't blow up the White House."

The big guy stared at her. "What are you talking about?"

"I'm talking about your kite, and the bomb you have in there."

The big guy shook his head. "Is no bomb."

"Then your missile. Or whatever you were planning to use."

He was still shaking his head. "You are fools," he said. "You are children. You do not know what you have done."

"Well, we'll see about that when the police get here," said Suzana, pulling her phone out of her pocket.

"No!" said a voice. We looked over and saw Cameron running toward us, waving his arms. "Don't call the police!"

"Why not?" she said.

"Because we had it totally wrong," he said, puffing to a

stop. "I tried to tell you on the phone but the battery died. I ran all the way here to tell you. We're totally wrong!"

"What are you talking about?" I said. I pointed at the two Gadakistanis. "Aren't these guys—"

"These are the *good guys*, Wyatt! The bad guys are at the White House right now, and they're about to kill the president!"

CHAPTER

21

We were gathered around Cameron—me, Suzana, Matt, and Victor, all of us totally confused, along with the big guy, who looked mad. He was still wearing a headset with a microphone. He had a miniature portable TV clipped to his belt, showing the C-SPAN broadcast of the White House press conference with the president and the Gadakistan leader, Brevalov. The little Gadakistani guy was still lying on the ground, moaning; his headset was on the ground next to him.

The lunatic taxi driver was sitting on the ground also not looking great, having now been both Raptored *and* landed upon. He was staring at me, but for the moment not saying anything. I think the big guy made him nervous. I wasn't paying much attention to him, because like everybody else I was trying to follow what Cameron was saying.

What he told us was this:

After the Gadakistani guys captured him, he managed to make friends with them, and the reason—believe it or not—was Worm Wrangler, which is this phone game that has like seventeen thousand levels and is very addictive. The Gadakistanis—whose names were Woltar (big guy) and Lemi (little guy)—had discovered Worm Wrangler on Matt's phone. They'd never seen it before, which tells you how backward Gadakistan must be, and they started playing it, and of course they got addicted. By the time Suzana and I rescued Matt and they captured Cameron, they were totally obsessed with it. But they were stuck on this one level (the one where the worm is attacked by vampire snails) and it was making them crazy because they couldn't get past it. So they broke down and asked Cameron to help them, and fortunately he had beaten that level so he showed them what to do. They were really grateful, and that kind of broke the ice.

They told Cameron they were sorry about capturing him, and they would let him go soon, but they couldn't risk having the police find them before they completed their mission.

Cameron asked what the mission was, and they said they were members of the Dragon Head rebel group, and they'd been sent to save the U.S. president.

"That's what they were trying to do just now when you guys showed up," said Cameron. "They were trying to keep the president from being assassinated."

"Assassinated by who?" said Suzana.

"Brevalov," said Cameron. He pointed at the little television, which was showing the press conference, with the president standing next to a guy with a beard. "Except that guy *isn't* Brevalov. That's a guy who had plastic surgery to look like Brevalov. He was sent here on a suicide assassination mission by the real Brevalov."

"Why?" said Victor. "I thought Brevalov was friendly to the United States."

"NO!" said the big guy, Woltar. "He pretends to like America, but he hates America. He is crazy. He wants to start war with America. He thinks many nations will join him. Crazy! We try to warn America, but nobody believes us. They think *we* are enemy. So we try to stop Brevalov. But now . . ." He pointed at Lemi, moaning on the ground. "Is no hope."

"How do we know you're telling the truth?" said Suzana.

"Suzana," said Cameron. "These are good guys. I believe them."

"You hardly know them!" said Suzana. "Just because they played Worm—"

"Google picture of Brevalov," interrupted Woltar.

"Why?" asked Suzana.

"Do it."

Suzana got out her phone and tapped the screen. A few seconds later she had an image of a bearded guy. "Okay," she said.

"Look at ear. On right side."

Suzana spread her fingers to zoom in on the picture. I leaned over to see. His ear looked normal to me.

"What about his ear?" said Suzana.

Woltar unclipped the portable TV and handed it to her. "Now look at this man who says he is Brevalov."

We all looked at the screen. It took a few seconds before they showed the bearded guy, but when they did, he turned to look left, and we could see his right ear clearly.

A little piece of the ear was missing. It wasn't much, but it was clear: There was a V-shaped notch.

"Is not Brevalov," said Woltar. "Is assassin."

"Oh, man," said Matt. "And we stopped these guys from stopping the assassin. We really screwed up."

My stomach felt like it had a hole in it, because in fact *I* was the one who'd stopped them. *Way to go, Wyatt! Way to yet again, somehow, some way, manage to make everything even worse.*

"How's he going to assassinate the president?" said Victor. "I mean, he couldn't bring a gun into the White House, could he?"

"No gun," said Woltar. "Snake."

"*What?*" said pretty much everybody at once.

"At end of press conference," said Woltar, "assassin will give president a gift. Is ceremonial Gadakistan wooden box. Inside box is Gadakistan mountain snake, deadliest snake in world. Very mean snake. When president opens box, it will bite him, and he will die in seconds." He looked at the TV screen. "Soon."

Now the hole in my stomach was the size of the Grand Canyon.

"We have to do something," said Suzana.

"We could call the police," said Matt.

"There's not enough time," said Suzana. "And they wouldn't believe us anyway."

"Then what?"

Suzana pointed to the dragon. "What were you going to do with the kite?" she said.

"We fly kite with Lemi inside. When kite gets near fence, Lemi pulls lever, releases rope. Then he flies kite like glider. It has special controls. He flies over fence."

"And he has the laser jammer to keep the missiles from shooting him down," said Victor.

"Yes," said Woltar. "He lands kite and stops assassin."

"Stops him how?" said Suzana.

"With throwing fork."

"With *what?*" said Suzana and I at the same time.

"Traditional Gadakistani hunting weapon," said Woltar. He went over to Lemi, the little guy, who was sitting up now, but still obviously in pain. Woltar leaned over and gently pulled something out of Lemi's waistband and brought it back to us. It was a heavy-looking fork with two prongs and a long handle.

"You *hunt* with that thing?" said Matt.

Woltar nodded. "Very deadly. Also efficient. Kill prey with it, then *eat* prey with it."

"So your friend"—Suzana pointed at Lemi—"was going to throw the fork at the fake Brevalov before he could release the snake on the president."

Woltar nodded. "Lemi is expert fork thrower. Was good plan." He shook his head. "No good now."

Everybody was quiet for a few seconds.

"No," said Suzana. "It's still a good plan. I'll fly the dragon."

Of *course* Suzana would volunteer to fly the dragon.

But Woltar was shaking his head again.

"No," he said. "You are too heavy. Weight makes dragon unstable. Must be somebody same weight as Lemi. Like him."

Woltar was pointing at me.

Suzana was looking at me.

They *all* were looking at me.

Here's the thing. I don't know how to fly a glider. I don't even like heights. I've thrown up on several roller coasters. Also, in case you haven't already figured it out, I am not the bravest person in the world. So I knew I was totally one hundred percent unqualified for this mission. It would be a disaster. The only intelligent thing for me to do was tell these people staring at me that I could not fly the dragon.

"Okay," I said. "I'll fly the dragon."

CHAPTER 22

Everything happened really fast. Woltar picked up Lemi's headset and put it on me. Then he lifted up the dragon and told me to get under it. It had an aluminum frame that formed a little cockpit. There were handles on the sides for holding on to the kite during the running takeoff, and a little seat to hop on when it (yikes!) left the ground. In front of me was a small windshield and the glider controls, which consisted of two levers and a red handle.

Woltar squatted on the ground and ducked his head (which is all of him that would fit) into the cockpit. He pointed to the red handle and said, "When I tell you, pull this to release rope." Then he pointed to the levers and said, "Pull left one, turn left. Pull right one, turn right."

Simple enough.

Then he pointed to something I hadn't noticed: duct-taped to the frame was the laser jammer.

"If missiles come," he said, "push button."

Oh, right. Missiles.

"How will I know if missiles are coming?"

"You will see them. And I will shout."

Okay, then.

"We must hurry. I will launch you now." He started to duck out of the cockpit, then ducked back in. "One more thing."

"What?" I said.

He reached in and tucked something heavy into my waistband.

The throwing fork.

"I don't know how to throw that thing," I said.

"You must try," he said.

"But I—"

"No more talk!" said Woltar. "We must go!"

He ducked back out of the dragon.

"I've never shot a gun," I said, to myself.

"Get ready!" I heard Suzana's voice coming from my right, outside the dragon. I grabbed the side handles and lifted the dragon. My legs felt shaky from fear, not from weight; the kite was amazingly light. I looked through the little windshield and saw the back of Woltar, jogging forward with the rope over his shoulder, taking out the slack.

My headset crackled, and I heard Woltar's voice: "Run!"

I started running, and just in time, because the rope slack was gone, and the dragon jerked forward. The cockpit was bouncing around and I couldn't keep my face in front of the windshield, so I was basically running blind. I heard shouting all around me—Suzana, Matt, Cameron, Victor, and a bunch of other people.

The dragon was moving faster, and I was starting to have trouble keeping up. I stumbled, almost fell.

Then two things happened, one right after the other.

The first was that the kite took off. Not gradually. Suddenly. So suddenly that the handles yanked my arms up and the kite almost took off without me before I managed to jump and pull myself up and slide back onto the seat. I felt the kite drop a little under my weight, then start to rise again. Now I could see out the windshield. Woltar, his back to me, was at the end of the rope, still running hard. I could hear him breathing in my headset. The guy was a beast.

The second thing you will not believe. The dragon suddenly jerked downward, so for a second my feet hit the ground again. I looked down.

"Thief!"

Yes! The maniac taxi driver was *still not giving up*. He had grabbed hold of the frame, so the dragon was dragging him along the ground. I guess he thought he could pull it down. It looked like he might.

But he couldn't. With Woltar the Beast pulling the rope, the kite started going back up. It was wobbling all over the place—Woltar was right about too much weight making it unstable. But it was still going up.

"Let go!" I yelled at the maniac.

"Thief!" he yelled. He was not letting go.

In a few more seconds he *couldn't* let go, because the dragon, still wobbling like crazy, had started gaining altitude pretty fast. I looked down between my legs and saw people on the Ellipse pointing up at us and shouting. They looked like they were a long way down.

And we were still rising. The higher we got, the stronger the wind blew. The dragon started zigzagging back and forth across the sky, with the taxi driver dangling underneath. I would probably have puked except I was too scared. We were so high up that I didn't want to look down. We were also so high up that the taxi driver had stopped calling me a thief and had switched to saying something in a foreign language. I think maybe he was praying.

And we were still going up.

And up.

And up.

The zigzagging was getting really bad. I grabbed the control levers and started pulling on them, trying to make it stop. I got it to be a little better, but we were still all over the place. The taxi driver was praying louder, and I didn't blame him, because we were really high up now and the zigzags were swinging him back and forth. He couldn't hold on forever.

Then I heard Woltar's voice in the headset. He was hoarse, gasping for air.

"Pull red handle! Pull red handle now!"

I looked at the handle, but I hesitated. I was scared to pull it.

"PULL RED HANDLE NOW!"

I reached down, grabbed the handle, and pulled. I think what I was thinking, if I was thinking anything, was: *Whatever happens next can't be as bad as this.*

I was an idiot.

CHAPTER 23

The first problem was, I couldn't really see anything. I mean, I could see *down*, but (a) it was scary to look down, because it showed how high up I was, and (b) looking down didn't tell me where I was going. But when I looked through the windshield, which was small, I mainly saw the sky, with occasionally a large object such as the Washington Monument whizzing past. I was holding tight to the levers, trying to control the zigzagging, but I was not having a huge amount of success.

"LEFT TURN!" Woltar shouted in my headset.

I pulled on the left lever.

"MORE LEFT!"

I pulled harder. The good news was, that stopped the zig-zagging. The bad news was, the dragon started to go into a spiral, which was seriously scary. Judging by his scream, the taxi driver did not care for it either.

"RIGHT! RIGHT! RIGHT!"

I yanked on the right lever. The spiral stopped.

"NOW STRAIGHT! STRAIGHT!"

I worked the levers, trying to keep the dragon straight, but it was tricky. I looked down and saw a road. Then a high fence.

The White House fence.

We were over the White House grounds.

We were also heading down. I flew over some grass, then a fountain, then more grass. I looked through the windshield, and now I could see it, straight ahead. The White House.

"LEFT! JUST A LITTLE!"

I tugged the left lever. When the dragon turned I could see a bunch of people on the left side of the White House. At exactly that instant I saw a flash of light.

"MISSILE! MISSILE! MISSILE!"

With Woltar shouting in my ear, I let go of the right control lever and pushed the jammer button hard with my thumb.

Two things about the missile:

1. It didn't come from the roof of the White House, which is where you would think an anti-aircraft missile would come from. It came from under the ground. It, like, erupted out of the lawn. I don't know what else they have under the White House lawn. I just know it's not a normal lawn.

2. It was really, really, *really* fast. It was so fast that it got from the lawn to the dragon in almost exactly the same amount of time it took my hand to get from the lever to the button.

Almost exactly, but not *exactly*, or instead of a live human telling this story, I (and the taxi driver) would be several million human smithereens scattered around the general Washington, D.C., area. I must have pressed the button at the last possible instant, because the missile flew over the dragon, missing us by *maybe* five feet as it roared past at a bajillion miles per hour.

"MISSILE!" Woltar yelled again.

I still had my thumb on the button, so the second missile

also missed, although it sounded even closer than the first one. The problem was, with my right hand on the jammer, I was not really in control of the dragon anymore, so we were zig-zagging like mad, not to mention losing altitude. I grabbed the handle again, but I couldn't regain control, and I couldn't see where I was going anyway. I heard a lot of shouting, which I figured was the press conference people. I'll be honest: At that point I wasn't really thinking about saving the president. I was just hoping I would get back on the ground alive.

I didn't see much of what happened next, because I was inside the dragon. But like just about everybody else in the world, I've seen the video, since there were a bunch of television news cameras there. It's pretty insane. The president is standing next to the guy pretending to be Brevalov, who's holding a wooden box, which he is just about to give to the president, when a guy in the crowd notices the kite coming and shouts. Everybody looks, and they see this large flying dragon with a spooky head wobbling across the lawn toward the White House with a guy hanging out the bottom. There's a lot of yelling and the Secret Service guys swing into action, with some of them forming a perimeter around the president and the fake Brevalov, and some of them running toward the dragon, pulling guns out of their jackets.

Then the first missile launches, and some people scream. Then the second missile goes off. More screams. Both missiles barely—I mean *barely*—miss the dragon and disappear into the distance. (It was later learned that one missile came down in the Potomac River; the other one demolished a fortunately unoccupied taco truck in Arlington, Virginia.)

By this point the scene is pretty much total chaos. The dragon is still coming, and people are running around shouting.

I need a bunch of words to describe what happens next, but in real time it takes a total of thirteen seconds.

First, a Secret Service guy, having seen the missiles miss, decides to shoot the dragon down. He's standing right in front of it, and he's in shooting position with both hands on the gun, which (I learned this later) is a Sig Sauer pistol that shoots .357 caliber bullets, which are big bullets.

Secret Service agents, especially the ones around the president, are excellent shots, and there is absolutely no doubt that this agent is going to blow a major hole in the dragon, and probably me. Except that just as he's about to pull the trigger the taxi driver finally loses his grip and falls, and his momentum carries him forward enough that he lands *right on the Secret Service agent.*

So it's a good thing he came along after all.

The sudden loss of weight causes the dragon to swoop violently up, which is fortunate because it causes two more Secret Service agents to miss me with their shots.

197

Unfortunately the swoop also causes me to lose my grip on the control levers. Then the dragon suddenly dives almost straight down. The front end hits the grass first and the whole dragon does a somersault, with people scattering out of the way.

And then, as the dragon completes a three-hundred-sixty-degree flip, a shape comes blasting out if it.

This is me. The dragon frame has basically turned into a catapult, and it is flinging me out through the kite skin and a good fifteen feet into the air on an arc that takes me over the perimeter of Secret Service guys surrounding the president and the fake Brevalov. There's a pretty famous picture of this, which you've probably seen. I'm frozen in midair, looking completely terrified, which I am; below me are four Secret Service guys, also frozen, looking up at me with these frowny, kind of puzzled expressions, like they're thinking, *They trained us for a lot of weird stuff in Secret Service school, but they did not prepare us for a kid to be vomited out of a flying dragon.*

What I wish I could say happens next is that I slam into the fake Brevalov and knock him out. But this is not what happens.

What happens is, I slam into the president of the United States of America.

And knock him down.

And break his collarbone.

Which is probably not what Mr. Barto had in mind back in the Miami airport when he gave us the lecture about how we had to be on our very best behavior as ambassadors representing Culver Middle School.

Okay, that's seven of the thirteen seconds. Here's what happens in the last six:

The president of the United States and I roll over a couple of times on the ground. Meanwhile the Secret Service guys are spinning around, lunging toward us, ready to swing into action, to save the president.

But the fake Brevalov is closer. He's lunging toward us, too. And he has the snake box in his hands. He's opening the lid. He's going to dump the snake—"Deadliest snake in world," said Woltar; "Very mean"—on the president. Also pretty much on me. I doubt the snake cares who it bites.

So I see the fake Brevalov and his snake box coming toward us—you can see this all on YouTube, in slow motion—and somehow, I will never know how, I remember the throwing fork. I yank it out of my pants and heave it with kind of a sideways motion at the fake Brevalov.

The fork totally misses the fake Brevalov.

It also, fortunately, totally misses the lunging Secret Service agents, who are right behind the fake Brevalov.

What the throwing fork hits, somehow, is: the snake.

You can also see this in slow motion on the video. It was later called, by Gadakistani experts, the greatest Gadakistani throwing fork throw ever thrown, although it was one hundred percent pure luck. In the video, you can see the deadly Gadakistan mountain snake coming out of the box with its mouth wide open, ready to strike me or the president with these long, sharp, mean-looking fangs. Then you see the fork coming from the other direction, spinning in the air but miraculously getting into exactly the right position so that one of the prongs goes right into the snake's open mouth, then comes out the back of the snake's head, and just like that the deadliest snake in the world got turned into a harmless snake kebab.

I didn't see any of that happen in real time. By the time that fork hit the snake I had two Secret Service agents who could probably be NFL linebackers landing on top of me and—I don't blame them a bit; they were trained to do this, and it was the absolute correct thing to do, considering what the situation looked like—knocking me unconscious with some kind of martial-arts blow to my head.

And that's the last thing I remember.

CHAPTER 24

I woke up in a bed in some kind of military hospital. I still don't know exactly where it was. I do know there were guards at the door and a lot of people in uniforms around.

After I woke up, two doctors came in and spent a long time checking me out and giving me tests to see if I had a concussion. I felt okay and kept trying to ask them questions, like could I talk to my parents, and was I in really bad trouble, and what was going to happen to me, stuff like that. But they wouldn't tell me anything.

After they left, a soldier brought me breakfast, which I figured meant I had been there overnight. I was starving

201

and ate the whole breakfast in maybe thirty seconds. After that, two people, a man and a woman, both wearing business clothes, came in and told me they were with the FBI, and they wanted to ask me "some questions."

It turned out that "some" meant "about 263 million." They wanted to know everything about how I ended up decking the president, starting basically with my birth. They were especially interested in everything I could tell them about Woltar and Lemi—how I met them, everything they did and said, why I was inside their dragon kite. They asked what I knew about the fake Brevalov. They wanted to know all about the throwing fork, and they had many, *many* questions about the laser jammer. They asked me the same questions over and over again, changing them just a little. Every now and then they would ask me if I was okay, and I'd say yes I was okay, but I wanted to talk to my parents. But they'd just go right back to asking me more questions.

After a couple of hours they left, and a soldier brought me lunch. When I finished eating, two new guys came in, both wearing suits. They didn't tell me who they were with, and they didn't answer any of my questions; they just asked me more questions, and more questions, and then more questions. By that point I was feeling like, okay, put me in jail or shoot me or whatever you're going to do, just *please stop asking me questions.*

Finally they left, and the doctors came back to check on me. They didn't tell me much, but it seemed like they had decided that I was basically fine.

Then they left, and I was finally alone. There was no clock, and I didn't have my phone, so I don't know how long I was alone, but it felt like hours. I tried to sleep, but I was too nervous, worrying about what was going on out there in the world, and what was going to happen to me.

Then the door opened. I was expecting that it would be either a soldier with dinner, or the doctors again, or, worst case, people in suits coming to ask me more questions and not tell me anything.

But it was none of those people.

It was the president of the United States.

With his arm in a sling.

"Hey, Wyatt," he said. "Thanks for saving me, but next time could you try to land on the bad guy?"

CHAPTER 25

o here's what had happened while I was in the hospital:

The flying dragon attack and the injury to the president immediately became the top news story in the world. Every television station showed the video in a loop pretty much nonstop.

The news media went nuts covering the story, with experts providing hour after hour of informed speculation, pretty much all of which was wrong. At first everybody focused on the flying dragon, which a lot of experts speculated was part of an assassination plot aimed at either the president or Brevalov, or both. There was no mention in any of the early reports about the deadly Gadakistan mountain snake.

I immediately became the most famous eighth-grader on the planet Earth, except for maybe Justin Bieber when he was thirteen. The only thing the FBI was saying about me was that I had been taken to an undisclosed location for questioning. There was a lot of expert speculation about how I might have been recruited to be a terrorist. There was also a lot of speculation about the identity of the man who fell from the dragon and landed on the Secret Service agent. The FBI said only that he also been taken to an undisclosed location for questioning.

In Miami, a giant crowd of news media people surrounded my house and pestered my parents for a statement about how their son came to be mixed up with what appeared to be a terrorist assassination plot. Finally my dad came to the door and told them that he and my mom didn't know anything except what they saw on television, and they were trying to make arrangements to fly to Washington, and they would appreciate it if the media would leave them alone. But the media kept ringing the doorbell and asking for statements, until finally my mom—I believe I have mentioned that she is Cuban—opened the door and broke my dad's golf umbrella in two by whacking it on the head of a Channel Seven TV reporter. This made international news, but also backed them off for a while.

While all this media speculating was going on, the FBI was conducting a really intense investigation, with help from the Secret Service, the CIA, and the Washington, D.C., police. They quickly picked up Suzana, Victor, Cameron, Matt, Woltar, and Lemi, who were identified by witnesses at the kite festival as having been involved in launching the dragon. They detained everybody—kids, teachers, and chaperones—who was part of the Culver class trip. They also picked up Mr. Barto, who had finally managed to talk the TSA into releasing him from custody at the Washington airport, only to be taken back into custody by four FBI agents and whisked off to an undisclosed location.

They questioned everybody, but the important people were Woltar and Lemi. They told the FBI about the fake Brevalov with the non-notched right ear, and they were convincing enough that the FBI decided to check it out. That was a good thing, because the fake Brevalov and his fake interpreter were already headed to Dulles International to get a flight out of the country. The FBI caught them at the airport. They refused to talk, but by then it was pretty clear that they were not who they claimed they were.

Meanwhile FBI crime-scene investigators were going

over the site of the dragon crash, and of course they found the corpse of the deadly Gadakistan mountain snake. Then they looked at a bunch of video in slow motion and saw how the fake Brevalov tried to dump the snake on the president just before I threw the throwing fork.

So it took a while, but they finally figured everything out and realized that Woltar, Lemi, and the rest of us were telling the truth. They reported everything to the president, who decided he needed to go on television and address the nation, to clear up all the rumors and assure America that everything was okay.

But first he wanted to thank me.

Which is how I ended up having a ten-minute conversation with the president, just the two of us. I don't remember that much of it; I was mainly happy I wasn't going to jail. The president said he would take me and my family and the whole Culver class on a personal tour of the White House after my parents got to Washington. I said a tour sounded great, assuming my mom didn't kill me first. He laughed. Because he didn't know my mom.

CHAPTER 26

A whole lot of stuff happened after that. In fact, a lot of stuff is still happening. I'll summarize the highlights:

- My mom did not kill me. I think she had been considering it, but a lot of people were telling her she must be very proud of me for saving the president, so she finally decided to go ahead and not kill me, although she told me that if I ever again did anything as stupid as attacking the White House in a kite, she definitely would.

- Woltar and Lemi got into trouble for violating a bunch of laws, including buying the stolen laser jammer. But as many people pointed out, they had to do these things because nobody believed them when they tried to tell the U.S. government about the assassination plot. The truth is, they were the real heroes, and in the end they were not charged with anything.

- On the other hand, the fake Brevalov and his fake interpreter were charged with a bunch of things. They haven't been tried yet, but they definitely will not be going back to Gadakistan any time soon.

- Speaking of Gadakistan: when people there found out that the real Brevalov had been lying about being friends with the United States, he got chased out of office by an angry mob. He wound up hiding in the mountains, and just recently there was a rumor that he died after he got bit by a snake. Guess what kind.

- The taxi driver turned out to be a guy from Nigeria named Ogochukwoo "Ogo" Adebayo. He was questioned at length by FBI agents, who ultimately decided that he had not done anything illegal except fall on a Secret Service agent, which was not really his fault. You will probably not be surprised to hear that when they told him he could go free, he asked them where I was, because *he still wanted his money.* I'm glad to report that he finally got it, from my dad, who added a twenty-dollar tip, which didn't seem like a lot to me after everything Ogo had been through. But Ogo was more than satisfied. He just wanted his money.

- Miss Rector and Mr. Barto were not thrilled when they found out all the stuff that Suzana, Matt, Cameron, Victor, and I did while we were supposed to be under their supervision. Mr. Barto was especially upset about us getting him busted by the TSA for the gun-shaped cigarette lighter. There was some talk of discipline, maybe even suspension. But in the end the school authorities decided that it wouldn't look right, punishing what the *Miami Herald*, in a front-page story, called "The Kids Who Saved The President." It helped that the president made good on his promise to host the whole class trip on a special tour of the White House, which was pretty cool except for the part where my mom decided to give the president, in the Oval Office, a lecture on all the things—she had an actual list, which she pulled out of her purse—that he was doing wrong. He took it pretty well and even joked that maybe he should appoint my mom to his cabinet. My dad and I gave each other a look that said *Don't give her any ideas.*

As for me, I have to say it was pretty great, being one of The Kids Who Saved The President. Suzana, Matt, Cameron, Victor, and I got a ton of attention—people wanting to have us on their television shows, interview us for newspapers and magazines, stuff like that. We got all these offers of free stuff, including trips to Disney World. People wanted our

210

autographs. Our faces were everywhere. In a couple of hours I went from two Twitter followers (Matt and Cameron) to 4.7 million followers, even though in my entire Twitter career I had tweeted a total of three things, one of which was actually a retweet of a fart joke from Cameron. It didn't matter. Everybody *loved* us.

So that was all pretty exciting. But sometimes it was also kind of awkward for me, because I was the one who flew the dragon, so I got more attention than anybody else. I got called "hero" a lot, which really bothered me, because I knew it wasn't true. Heroes are brave people who do dangerous things on purpose. Everything I did was a result of being either completely terrified or unbelievably lucky. I always told the interviewers this, and I always stressed how most of the credit belonged to Woltar and Lemi and the other kids, especially Suzana. But I think it bothered Suzana, me being singled out. She never said anything, but I think deep down inside she wished it had been her flying the dragon.

Anyway, after a couple of weeks of complete craziness we started settling back into the normal routine at Culver Middle. That's where I am now, getting near the end of eighth grade. The kids at Culver aren't talking about what happened in Washington much anymore. Everybody's more interested in stuff like who's going to what high school. Also we talk a lot about the eighth-grade prom. Its official name is the

Eighth Grade Banquet, I think because the school administrators think we're too young to have a prom. But everybody calls it the prom.

You don't have to have a date for the prom. Everybody goes, and a lot of kids go solo. Pretty much all the nerds do. So I figured I would. I'd hang around with Matt and Cameron and the other nerds, and it would be fine.

Except the more I thought about it, the more I realized I didn't want to go solo.

I wanted to go with Suzana.

The problem was that if I asked her to the prom, I figured there was an excellent chance she'd say no, because even though she acted friendly to me in school—a lot friendlier than she was before we went to Washington—she was back to spending most of her time inside the Hot/Popular clot, which included J.P. Dumas, who was still tall, and still Suzana's boyfriend, as far as I could tell.

But I didn't know for sure.

And the only way to find out was to ask her.

It took me five days to work up enough courage to do it. I knew exactly where Suzana would be between classes, and when the bell rang I would sprint to a spot by the cafeteria and sort of hover around trying to look casual until Suzana walked past, usually in the middle of a pack of hot girls, and instead of walking up and saying, "Suzana, will you go to the prom with me?" I'd wave a stupid little wave and say, "Hey." That was what came out Monday, Tuesday, Wednesday, and Thursday: "Hey."

So it came down to Friday. The bell rang; I sprinted to my cafeteria hover spot and tried to look casual. The hot-girl pack came drifting my way, Suzana in the middle. *This is it,* I told myself. *Now or never.*

I opened my mouth.

And I said, quote, "Hey."

Idiot.

Suzana waved and kept walking.

I stood there, feeling like the world's biggest loser, watching the hot girls walk away.

Then Suzana stopped.

She turned around and walked back to me.

"Wyatt," she said. "Do you have something you want to say to me?"

"No," I said, adding, "Yes."

You are SUCH an idiot.

"Okay," she said. "What is it?"

"Um," I said, getting off to a solid start. "I was thinking. I mean wondering. I mean I was thinking about if maybe you . . . I mean, I realize probably not. You and J.P. are still dating, right? I mean each other?"

"Wyatt," she said. "Are you trying to ask me to go to the prom?"

"Um," I said. "Can I ask you if you would *like* me to ask you to the prom? I mean, how do you think you'd feel about it? If I asked you?"

She stared at me for several seconds.

"Wyatt," she said. "If you *don't* ask me to the prom, I will kick your butt. I will hong fo you right through the cafeteria wall, here and now. And you know I can."

I knew she could.

"Okay," I said. "Will you go to the prom with me?"

"I would love to," she said.

And then she kissed me right on the mouth.

She had to lean down a little to do it.

But not too much.

I'm definitely catching up.